HER:A PSYCHOLOGICAL THRILLER

BRITNEY KING

WWW.BRITNEYKING.COM

ALSO BY BRITNEY KING

HER: A PSYCHOLOGICAL THRILLER

BRITNEY KING

COPYRIGHT

HER is a work of fiction. Names, characters, places, images, and incidents are products of the author's imagination or are used fictitiously and are not to be construed as real. Any resemblance to actual events, locales, organizations, persons, living or dead, is entirely coincidental and not intended by the author. The scanning, uploading, and distribution of this book without permission is a theft of the author's intellectual property. No part of this publication may be used, shared or reproduced in any manner whatsoever without written permission except in the case of brief quotations embodied in critical articles and reviews. If you would like permission to use material from the book (other than for review purposes), please contact http://britneyking.com/contact/ Thank you for your support of the author's rights.

Hot Banana Press
Cover Design by Britney King LLC
Cover Image by Britney King LLC
Copy Editing by Librum Artis Editorial Service
Proofread by Proofreading by the Page

First Edition: 2019
ISBN 13: 9781797040912

britneyking.com

This is not for you.

"The truth will set you free, but first it will piss you off." — Joe Klaas

PROLOGUE

Now

I wish someone had told me: worry is a waste of time. The real troubles of your life will be things that never even bothered to cross your mind.

Nine months, three days, and nineteen hours, I've lived down the street from her. If you really think about it, a person can do a lot in nine months. They can gestate a fetus and deliver it safely into the world, and they can also plant roots and create an entirely different life altogether. That's what she did.

Not that I realized it at the time, but in essence, that's what she helped me to do, too. What's good for the goose is good for the gander, as they say. Only she isn't a bird. She can't just fly away, the way she thinks she can.

She thinks she can migrate, start a new life elsewhere, someplace where she can be whatever she wants to be. But she's forgetting two things: wherever you go, there you are. Also, there are people like me.

When I moved to this boring, homogeneous, monotonous

little town, I did so with one intention and one intention only: to have a nice life. A quiet life.

That's not how it played out. Not even close.

First, it was good. And then it got bad before it got good again.

I met her and life changed.

What can I say? I got swept up in it. She makes it easy. Her, with her impractical shoes and her perpetually sunny nature. For me, she always has felt a bit like spring in the middle of winter. She was then, and still is to me now, just about the most wonderful thing in the world.

But there's something to be said for that. Something I hadn't realized at the start. It was a new experience for me, and I felt dizzy for a while. Like most things, dizziness fades. And then, it dawns on you, the relationship you have in your mind is profoundly different from the one you actually have.

Of course, it takes precious time before you figure this out. Only by then, it's too late. By then, desire has already taken you to the darkest edges of humanity. It's a special place in the deepest recesses of hell, let me tell you. That's when you realize what they say is true: Every love affair has its rituals—and you always kill what you love in the end.

On so many occasions, this could have taken a different route. She could have proven me wrong, and yet so many times she took exactly the route I predicted. We all make choices. She made hers. I made mine. Those choices have consequences. I'd like to think I've been lenient with her, far more lenient than I should have been.

So, that's how I've found myself here, at the end that's really a beginning. Here, in her kitchen, sitting at her bar, turning the knife over in my hands. All the while knowing that what awaits me upstairs will not be easy.

It's okay.

No one ever said revenge was easy. Just sweet. One of her favorite sayings. She was wrong about a lot of things—me, for one

—but *that*, well, that she was right about. Revenge is surprisingly sweet. It's clear in the steadiness of my breath, in the clarity that has washed over me. My hands don't even shake.

There are eleven steps to the top of the stairs. I've counted.

Her death will not be random. A crime of passion, they'll call it. Although it will not be done in the heat of the moment, the way one might suspect. No. This is a scene I've played out in my mind, hundreds, if not thousands, of times. I knew it wouldn't be easy. She is my friend, my only friend. She prefers it that way.

Yes, I am aware of how pathetic this sounds. I wish I knew how to make you understand. It's just...well, I've never been very good with words. That's her gift. Mine is asking questions. Maybe I should start there. Have you ever met someone you know is absolutely terrible for you but for whatever reason, combined with all the mysteries of the universe, you just can't help yourself? Well, for me, that person is her.

I can't help myself. She's black magic and at the same time the air I need to breathe. Which is why I was careful to prepare for any and all setbacks. Setbacks have always been our specialty.

I finish off my Danish, careful to savor it in the way that she would appreciate. Next, I slip off my shoes, and leave them neatly by the door, just as I have countless times before, on more pleasant visits.

To outsiders, her death will come as a shock. Obviously, not for long. I've accounted for this. Which is to say, I don't plan to stick around. Statistics show most victims know their perpetrators. Murder is astonishingly predictable. Since the beginning of time we've been sleeping, eating, having sex, and murdering each other. And not necessarily in that order.

Why no one ever sees these things coming is beyond me.

She really should have seen it coming.

Trust is a slippery thing though, isn't it? Intangible, I've come to find. It doesn't matter how smart your brain is. The heart is a different organ entirely. At least, this is the only logical explanation I can come up with as to why the truth so often remains elusive even when it's dangled right in front of us. It isn't logical at all. For so long, I thought if I just tried hard enough, I could make this work. There's a price for that kind of stupidity. And believe me, I paid it.

Now, it's her turn.

You live and you learn, I suppose. And let me tell you, I have learned...

At the top of the stairs, I will find her in her bed, third door to the right. By this time of night, she will be sleeping on her side, covers pulled halfway up. Her expression will be slack, but peaceful, for even in sleep women like her know only ease.

On the left side of the four-poster bed, is a nightstand. On top of the nightstand rests her Bible, the cell phone she'll never reach, a glass of water she'll never drink, the reading glasses she doesn't want anyone to know she needs.

I will attack from the right, stabbing her six times. I've mapped it out. Six stab wounds, one for each of the ways she has wronged me. In reality, it doesn't take that much to kill a person. She probably knows this better than anyone. And if not, just in case, I want to make sure.

CHAPTER ONE

SADIE

Then

Bone slams into pavement. The thud reverberates between my ears for several seconds before I see what caused it. Not that I have to look to know what has happened. What I hear is loud and clear. It's vertebrae pouring into the asphalt, breaking one by one at first, and then at last, a final crack.

First, a whooshing sound is registered. Afterward, gasping. *He isn't breathing,* someone calls out, and I feel myself being drawn in the direction of the mess, until I'm near the center. Stepping over a trail of blood that oozes down the sidewalk, I perch upward onto my tippy toes to get a better look.

Despite the flurry of activity, no one panics. All around me people continue on with their day. Bizarrely, most of them don't even stop what they are doing to see what's going on. The ones who do, do either one of two things: they pull out their phone to capture the moment, or they look to the person next to them as a cue for what to do. At the heart of it all, a man lies on the ground. A woman is hunched over him. She's performing CPR.

Upon closer inspection, I realize that the man sprawled out on the pavement is Creepy Stan. I know Stan. Everyone knows Stan. He works here. He bags groceries and has a penchant for saying wildly inappropriate things to female customers. Everyone overlooks it on account of his disability. Most of us avoid him all together.

But not her. She pumps Creepy Stan's chest as though her life depends on it. Although her hair shields the majority of her face, what I can see of her profile seems somewhat familiar. Mentally, I try to place her but can't.

Another bystander checks Stan's pulse. His expression causes the woman to work harder. "Help is on the way," someone says.

He just went down, a man says.

I think he tripped on the curb, an old lady says.

I saw him clutch his chest, someone else says.

This is why you can never trust eyewitness accounts.

I wonder if Stan can hear them. I assume not. His eyes are fixed straight ahead on the cloudy gray sky. It's almost poetic the way he watches the heavens. He doesn't blink. Blood pools around his head in a kidney-shaped pattern before flowing outward onto the pavement. My stomach barrel rolls. Blood and death and emergencies are not my strong suit. Too many memories. It's scary how fast the mind can travel.

Finally, paramedics arrive. Three men and one woman spill out of the fire truck. They move with purpose, almost in formation.

Stan isn't dead. He isn't breathing, but they bag him, and the good news is, at least he has a pulse. We all watch in unison as they deftly log roll him onto a spinal board before securing him onto the stretcher.

The crowd breathes a collective sigh of relief when the ambulance doors close and then they clap for the woman. When she turns in my direction, I realize I know her. It's Ann Banks. Internet celebrity. Best-selling author. Self-help guru. The kind of woman that puts all the mixed up puzzle pieces of the world in a neat little row. She has the ability to make you see the big picture. This is what they say each week, anyway, on her number one podcast. The book reviews. Her followers. They say she can change your life. As for what I think...well, the jury is still out.

A woman pulls her into an embrace. Cheers erupt, growing louder. It's a fucking moment, to be sure. "You're a hero," the old lady tells her. She smiles and says it was nothing.

CHAPTER TWO

HER

You're going to want to know who I am. You're going to want to know a lot of things about me. I don't want you to worry. We'll get there. In time, I assure you, you'll know everything there is to know.

Well, perhaps not *everything*. There is beauty in the ambiguous. You should keep that in mind.

If you ask me, there's far too little mystery left in the world. It's something I've often found interesting in my line of work. Everyone wants answers. So few want to work for them. There's something equally pleasant and terrifying in the unexplainable isn't there?

It makes sense, I suppose. Isn't that what we're all looking for? A little bit of magic. Something that sweeps in and takes us over. That is, until we find it and it terrifies us. We can't help ourselves. We pick it apart. We run it into the ground. *Tell me about yourself,* we say—to lovers, to friends, to everyone. *I need to understand. I need to see if who you are fits in with how I need you to be.*

It's a shame we feel the need to know every little thing. Because, and this is where I'd like to warn you, knowing every little thing is dangerous. Knowing every little thing is like asking for a cup of poison and drinking one tiny sip at a time. It'll kill you slowly. But it kills you nonetheless.

So, before I tell you about me, first, I should probably tell you about *her*. It's impossible to know me—to truly understand me—without knowing about her. She is the reason for everything I do, after all. From the get-go, from the first time I laid eyes on her, my whole life became about her. This is what happens when you love a person; when you truly love them.

Shakespeare said: Love is smoke and is made with the fume of sighs. *A madness most discreet.* Smart fellow, he was. Love makes me do things. Mad things. Bad things. Morally corrupt things.

It's all for her. This time was no different…

The way he looked at her as she spoke was unnerving. That in and of itself was nearly enough. But no, he couldn't stop with his eyes. He had to go and touch her. Not just her cart, but her things —*her person*. He rested his hand on her shoulder. He was so close that she could feel his hot, stinky breath on her face as he spoke. He told her she was pretty. *Pretty.* Not beautiful. Not stunning. Just pretty.

He didn't stop there. He made the mistake of letting his hand trail lower. She isn't the kind of woman that allows that. No funny business with her. He should have known better. I have a feeling now he does.

CHAPTER THREE

SADIE

I t is the Friday before Thanksgiving. I've packed my cart full of items to make a traditional meal, the one I'd made every year since Ethan and I'd become engaged, the one I no longer need to make anymore. It's just another thing taken from me. The list as long as the one in my hand.

It was sort of a last minute decision, coming here. A real recipe for disaster. But you never quite know these things beforehand though, do you?

If I had known I was going to meet someone, someone that would change my life, I would have dressed better and maybe combed my hair. I certainly wouldn't have thrown on yoga clothes, clothes too small and too old for such an occasion. To be honest, I'm only one step above leaving the house in my pajamas. I didn't, of course. I've lost a lot of things—I revel in the fact that at least my pride is only halfway out the door.

Still, cooking was a bad idea. I can see that now. But without a job, and with nothing to do other than twiddle my thumbs, it's not like I have a ton of other options.

I read a quote on Instalook this morning that said it's important to hang on to things that mattered. To act "as if." *Fake it till you make it*, or something like that.

I am working on it. Believe me. I'm possibly halfway there. I managed to get out of bed. I managed to put the key in the ignition, to open the garage, to put the car in reverse, and to drive to the supermarket. Baby steps.

Of course, I understand at the level that one understands these kinds of things that life has to go on. I understand there are things to live for. Or rather— at least if I hang on, there will be.

Revenge being one of them. *The best revenge is living well.* I have plans for that. Or I plan to have plans for that. Someday soon. *Maybe tomorrow.* Like I said, baby steps.

Today, I have plans to cook. Because knowing what you want and doing something about it are two different things entirely. The book on my nightstand says you can fake emotions outwardly, but only a true master can do it internally. It says: You can fool everyone else. But rarely yourself.

I'm not sure I buy that. I'm certainly not fooling anyone in this grocery store, that's for sure. I see the way they look at me. Which is why I'm not sure how long I've been standing in the same place. Maybe I've been in aisle four consulting this list for five minutes. Maybe it has been five hours. I have no idea. This is how life is now. Not that it matters. With nothing to break up my days, no one to be in a hurry for, no one to be accountable to, time expands into forever. I can do whatever I want now that it's just me, myself, and I. Ah, freedom. It's not even half as lovely as I'd thought it'd be.

It's evident in the way I am staring at words on a page, words that have lost their meaning, when I glance up, and what little wind I have in my sails is knocked out of me. *Shit.* I avert my gaze to the disaster headed my way and say a silent prayer that I'm doing as Ethan says—imagining things.

But no. When I look up, what I see is real, and she is, in fact, coming down the aisle toward me. It's all I can do to study my list and pray, pray, pray that she moves along.

Obviously, she doesn't. Instead, her far too cheerful voice reaches into the depths of my soul and gives it a slight tug. She doesn't even have to speak for me to understand the power and the pull she could execute over my life, if I let her.

"Excuse me?" she says, forcing me to acknowledge her. I shouldn't be surprised. I suppose this meeting was inevitable. This is a small town. Not that small really in terms of size, just small-minded. I knew I'd run into her eventually. But I've done well for myself; I've managed to avoid it for months. *Months*. It helps if you hardly leave the house—and yet here we are.

"Ma'am?" Her voice is hurried. Almost desperate.

A smile pulls at the corners of my lips. That's how bad I must look. She actually just called me *ma'am*. The word feels like shards of glass running across my skin. I should have known. She knows how to cut deep, this one.

Not that I know for sure or anything. It's just an assumption. I don't know her. Not really. "Do you know where the gluten-free aisle is?"

"Aisle six," I answer. It is a simple exchange. A basic question with a standard answer. And still, I can't make myself look at her straight on, peeking instead through the bangs that hide my eyes, my head tilted upward only slightly. In time I will learn—women like her despise meekness as much as they prey upon it.

She reaches out and balances herself on my cart. "Thank you," she exhales softly. "You saved me...I got halfway home and real-ized I'd forgotten the one thing I'd come for. And I'm afraid I've worn the wrong shoes."

My eyes land on her heels. She is right. No one in this town shops in shoes like that. No one except for her.

She shifts and finally, I steal a glance at her. A voice laced with that kind of charm does not a forgettable face make. Fierce red hair, not a strand of it out of place, striking eyes. Tall and lean.

The same as in the parking lot. But also, different. Not from here obviously, but then no one really is.

"I should have known you'd have the answer," she says, motioning toward my cart. My eyes follow, spotting the gluten-free crackers I don't recall tossing in. Some things are automatic. Grief hits me at my kneecaps, and suddenly I am standing in the ocean, the waves threatening to pull me under.

"Two aisles that way," I manage. "About a quarter of the way down."

"Thanks," she replies, her voice laced with cheer. Suddenly, I'm not sure whether I want to throat punch her or become her. No one is *that* friendly. Not even here. That's not to say everyone is unfriendly. I know what that kind of thinking can do. Ann's number one best seller told me that much. *Mindset is everything.*

Framing is important. *They aren't rude, Ann. Just too hurried, too caught up in themselves to bother with manners.* "You're a lifesaver," she offers.

My palms begin to sweat. When I look down I am surprised to see I am white-knuckling the cart. In her books she says we hold too tight to simple things, inanimate things, when our lives feel like they're spinning out of control.

"We're fairly new in town," she tells me proudly, as though this is something to be proud of. "I'm hosting a dinner party tonight… and my husband informed me at the last minute—of course—that one of the guests has dietary issues."

I look away. She reminds me of someone I might have become if I hadn't landed here too soon.

"You look familiar," she remarks, almost cautiously. "Do I know you from somewhere?"

My pulse quickens. "I don't think so."

She studies me carefully. I hate every millisecond of it. Suddenly, her eyes widen as recognition takes hold. She gets paid well to read people. I am not the exception to the rule.

All I can do is grip the cart, and hold on tight as everything goes to shit.

"Wait. I think maybe you live on our street." A smile plays upon her face. "Penny Lane. Yes, that's it. You live on Penny Lane."

"Oh—right," I stutter. I can see she is grateful to have solved the puzzle. "Penny Lane…that's me."

"I have to apologize," she tells me. "I've been meaning to get down there to introduce myself. I hate to make excuses—but with the move and with the holidays coming…well, I've been a little distracted." Finally, she extends her hand. "I'm Ann."

Her grip is warm and friendly, welcoming. The opposite of who I hoped she'd be. She's a master of reinvention. It never looked so good on anyone as it does her. Something I'd learn more of in time.

"Sadie."

"Tell me, what do people do around here, Sadie? For fun? We've lived here a few months and still—for the life of me—I can't figure it out."

The thing about Ann is she has elaborate ways of saying almost everything. She's a writer. Basically, she lies for a living. She's very good at it. Everyone says so.

"I don't know about anyone else," I say glancing around the store. "Me, I read, mostly," I add because despite my attire I'm pretty sure she isn't expecting me to say yoga.

"How wonderful." It's nice that she leaves it at that. She doesn't tell me that she, too, is an avid reader. But I guess the most important things we keep close to our chests.

"Do you have plans tonight?"

I cock my head and try to come up with something, with anything.

"I'll take that as a no," she quips. "This dinner party I'm hosting…a couple of neighbors are joining us…so you really must come."

"I—"

"Appetizers are served at six. Dinner is at seven. We're at 22243."

I want to accept her invitation. Just weeks before, I would have killed for it. "I really wish I could," I say, apologetically. "But I have all of this cooking to do."

Her expression goes blank for a second, and then there is something else, almost like a gate between us has closed. Whatever she is thinking, whatever I have said, the shift is palpable. She straightens her back and takes two steps forward. "No pressure. But if you can stop by, we'd love to have you."

"Thank you," I say, swinging my cart to the right. I have to get out of here before I mess anything else up. Some things you can't undo. "It was nice to meet you."

She nods and I nod. I would curtsy if it meant extinguishing the look of disappointment on her face. Ann Banks isn't the kind of woman who is familiar with rejection. She's said so herself. That's why she's so successful.

"A pleasure," she replies. "It's been harder than I thought to get to know people in this town."

I offer a tight smile. It's the best I can manage. How cute that she wants to be relatable. How very like her.

"Oh—and it's nice to know—the whole gluten issue isn't just made up."

"That's the thing…" I reply. "I'm starting to think it might be."

"I hope I'll see you again," she says.

I nod. *You will. My future happiness depends on it.*

Her features soften as she looks back over her shoulder. "This evening would be lovely."

"I'll try my best."

And just like that, we officially meet. A chance encounter that was fated to happen. It was less painful than I thought. All things considered. Conversation flowed. An invitation was extended. Neither of us mentioned what just happened in the parking lot. Ann isn't like that. She pushes onward. Onward toward her perfect new home, with her perfect husband and her perfect children. I leave the grocery store, like Ann says in her book and all over the internet, faking it until I make it. The thought makes me smile. I don't know what kind of person meets a stranger in a supermarket and invites them to their home straightaway. But as it turns out, Ann Banks is exactly that kind of person.

CHAPTER FOUR

SADIE

I'm loading the bags in my car, wondering what I was thinking. Even on a binge, I could never eat all of this. Even if I could, I can't afford it. Not now.

I take a deep breath. Ann's book says breath is one of our most important assets. Seems like a simple concept to me, but people pay her good money for such simplicity—reminding me that common sense isn't always common practice. Anyway, I breathe and I remind myself that my intentions were pure. The point was —to do normal people things. Things like cooking and making friends in the grocery store. Just in case my husband shows up. Which he probably won't. But just in case.

I want him to see that despite whatever has happened, I can be the woman he fell in love with again. She's still me. I'm still her.

Speaking of, I check the time, which is really an excuse to see if he's called or texted. He hasn't.

It isn't until I go to lift the last of the bags into the trunk, that I see it. Like a bad omen, on the edge of my periphery. A kitten as gray as the day, as gray as my mood, is crouched next to my tire. It's a tiny thing, scraggly and so dirty that at first glance, I almost mistake it for a piece of discarded trash. Squatting down, I speak softly. *"Hey there."*

As I move closer, I expect it to cower. It only blinks. I've always found cats interesting. Ethan is allergic. They carry disease, my mother always said. Not that she ever let me close to one. *Better to be safe than sorry.*

I'm hoping it will run. But it isn't scared. It doesn't move. It just peers up at me. It doesn't even make a sound, and for a moment I consider that it's just another one of those illusions I've been accused of having. Maybe it's hurt. It's chilly out, and the thing is so tiny. I lean in close, checking for visible injuries. Maybe it's been hit.

No. It looks fine to me.

My heartbeat cranks up a level. In a crisis, I'm amazing. It's the little things I can't manage. My husband used to tell me this all the time. I push myself up and search the lot. I don't know what to do. I can't very well back out with it under my tire, so I turn back and try nudging it out with my foot. *Go on*, I say. But nothing happens. It doesn't move.

I nudge it again, this time a little harder, until finally it makes a faint squeaking sound. Still, it stays put.

Again, I search the lot. There's a part of me that thinks maybe Ann Banks will materialize and fix this too. But even I know my luck isn't that far-reaching.

Quite the opposite. Instead, it feels like I've landed in one of those terrible animal commercials you see on late night TV. In the early days, Ethan and I used to watch those infomercials together. He said it made him feel like his problems weren't so bad, considering the alternative. He liked the emotion. I just liked the music.

Fuck, I think, throwing my hands up. I realize I can't just leave it there without it going splat for the next person that pulls in. That's a good way to ruin a person's day, for sure. When I look up two women have stopped and are staring. I crack my knuckles one by one, and they go on their merry way. I can do crazy really well, or so says my husband.

I'm not even a softie, and yet, I can't force my foot to connect with it again.

Perfect. Now, it looks like I have both food and a kitten I don't need, and if only there were a two for one shelter that would accept them both, all of my problems would be solved.

Almost.

I spot my husband's scarf in the backseat. In an instant, the decision is made. This is how I'll rid myself of it. This is how I let go. Little by little, piece by piece. I'll save the cat and the stranger from their respective bad days with the scarf, and then I'll toss it. Easy-peasy. It'll save me hours anyhow, no longer sitting in the car, crying into it, long after the engine has stopped running.

I bring it to my face and inhale deeply. *His scent still lingers on it.* It's hard to erase that. *Oh well.* One less reminder of what used to be but no longer is.

There are little pieces of him everywhere, landmines left for me to trip over.

Speaking of landmines, I recall the old towel in the trunk left there from our last beach trip, and I decide I should cover the seat, in the event that he does come back. Ethan is deathly allergic to cats. Probably better not to take the risk. As I shake it out, grains of sand dust the pavement. Memories follow suit. Although, that beach trip was months ago now, for me, it could have just as well been yesterday.

It was one of my good days. I'll never forget how it felt to have the sun and my husband's grace shine upon me. Or the manner in which we laid side by side on our backs, soaking it in. We listened to the waves grow closer and closer, both of us careful to keep our eyes steady on the birds overhead. I realize now this is just my version of that day, of course. It's likely he was plotting his escape even back then. They say a person does, at least dozens of times, before they actually make their break. Separation never comes as a shock to the one doing the leaving.

The memory is as clear as ever today; it's the visceral kind. The kind that hits you out of nowhere. The kind that's good enough to bottle and sell.

Birds squawked, children played, we stared straight up at the sky, both too content and too afraid to break the spell. It feels like a dream looking back. One good day sliced into a reel of a bunch of shitty ones. I can't blame him for wanting that version of us more than what we had become. I hold tight to that image too. Two lovers on the beach. Happy. Content. Safe.

Ethan's fingertips reached out and just barely brushed mine. I thought it was his way of telling me that things would be all right. But then, he couldn't have known that, could he?

My breath caught when he squeezed my pinky, just the tip. It felt like an unspoken promise. Afterward, he'd placed his hand over mine and rested it there, and it made me believe. It was all still there. Just buried. I could have stayed like that for hours. Forever, maybe. Ethan had a way of anchoring me to the earth. Otherwise, I would have been just as happy to float away.

CHAPTER FIVE

SADIE

Ann Banks saved a human. Big deal. I'm saving a cat. Something that sounded like a good idea until I'm firmly in the middle of it.

The thing is hell-bent on touching every surface in my car, thereby marking it as its own. *No good deed goes unpunished.* Great. I'll have to spend the rest of my life making sure I erase any evidence it was ever here. Ethan would kill me.

There's a veterinary place on the way home. I plan to drop it on the doorstep and hightail it outta there.

They say animals use more of their senses than humans, and I believe it. I can tell by the way it refuses to stay wrapped up in the towel despite how many times I place it there. Apparently, it doesn't appreciate the memory of that beach day as much as I do. *Stay,* I say. But it doesn't appear to understand English nor care to try and we're not even halfway there.

Cats carry disease. I can hear my mother's warning, clear as day. I mean, she's dead—but the dead can still be right.

When I was three I got ringworm from a neighborhood stray, and my mom had to shave my head. There are pictures some-where. People thought I was a cancer patient, which horrified my mother. That horror was only superseded when anyone assumed I was a boy.

I can recall in vivid detail the day she took me in for blood work just to make sure about the cancer. Ringworm could have been anything, she said. Technically. She sat me down and explained I might be dying. She was sorry, she said. She might have guessed wrong, and it might be too late. Even if it wasn't, we didn't have insurance, and cancer treatment is very expensive. So many lessons in one conversation. That was my mother.

The kitten yawns and stretches, and then it hops onto the seat and crawls into my lap. I move my hips, wiggling in my seat, anything to make it go back where it came from. It doesn't budge. Instead, it curls its tail under its body and settles in for a long winter's nap.

This forces me to steer with one hand while finagling the sleeve of my shirt over the other. It takes a bit of effort but eventually I'm able to lift the cat from my lap and once again place it back on the towel without it touching my skin.

We drive on.

When we arrive at the vet, I'm faced with the crippling reality that dropping it on the doorstep isn't going to be as easy as I'd envisioned in my mind. For one, there are windows everywhere. Two, people seem to come and go nonstop. I consider asking if any of them would like a free kitten. But they probably don't, and I hate rejection.

Ultimately, I go through the usual speech I have with myself before walking into a new experience. First, I count to ten. Then, I go through the alphabet. Somewhere around W, it dawns on me there's food in the back that will spoil. I finish on Z and suck it up. I wasn't always like this, in case you're wondering.

Ann Banks says in her book you should always look forward, never backward. This is useful in that I realize I should have considered what I'm going to say about the kitten on the way here instead of recounting my life story.

"It's never too late for a fresh start." She posted that on Instalook the other day.

I scoop the kitten up, along with the towel and cup it in my hands. "Sorry," I say. "But you're getting a fresh start."

You can't be a hero all the time.

Speaking of heroes, I could sure use one now. I'm not sure what I'm expecting when we reach the counter in the vet's office. Help, perhaps. What I'm not expecting is to be yelled at. Apparently I wasn't supposed to move the kitten. Apparently, its mother might have come back for it, and apparently I have ruined everything, including the circle of life.

Never mind that it was under my tire.

The technician tells me firmly that I can't leave the cat there. He informs me they are a business, not an animal shelter. I ask him what I should do. It's dehydrated, he says. And only about three weeks old. Which means it'll have to be bottle feed for a few weeks. It needed at least three weeks longer with its mother before it would be ready to survive on its own. I can take it to the shelter, he says. But they'll probably put it down.

"As in kill it?" I ask. It doesn't feel like a stupid question until it's out in the open and I see his expression. It's common sense; that's the way he looks at me. He doesn't understand why I don't know these things, so I assure him I'll make it a point to put nature on the list of things I need to learn.

I can't take it home, I say. And then, I tell him that my husband is allergic, as though this will explain everything.

He doesn't offer a response. Instead, after a rather intense stare down—maybe we're having a contest to see who will be the first to blink, and maybe we aren't—he asks if there's anything else he can help me with.

For the record, I won.

"I can't keep the cat," I repeat. I nod toward the veterinary symbol painted on the wall. "What about the Hippocratic oath?"

He sighs heavily. "It's not the same."

31

"Well, it should be," I say peering at the cat. "What happened to: To protect and to Serve?"

He's still not amused. "Also, not the same."

The standoff continues. I consider for a second just bolting. He sees me considering it. Maybe this is why he backtracks. Maybe it's because he sees how naïve I am. He tells me, if we get some weight on her, get her healthy; she will fare better at the shelter. Her odds of being adopted are better if she's cute and cuddly, he assures me. If I'm willing to foot the bill, they can care for her until she's old enough to eat on her own.

I don't ask how much this will cost, even though my mind is screaming that I should.

I simply hand over my credit card. The one reserved for emergencies. The one I'm well aware my husband will kill me for using.

CHAPTER SIX

SADIE

I arrive exactly on time. The whole ordeal with the kitten has turned me off to cooking, and since I can't go without eating, I figure I might as well take Ann Banks up on her invitation.

I wasn't going to. I am not very good with people I don't know. Come to think of it, not so good with the ones I do know, either.

Tonight is the first time in a long time, since *before*, since long before that, truthfully, that I've made any kind of effort. Even so, it is evident right away it wasn't enough. To say that I am out of place would be an understatement. I am out of place. My flat, mousy brown hair has nothing on the women here. They're well put together, with their cultivated, salon-colored, cut, and styled tresses. It's like a fucking shampoo commercial. Except that I am the only one twenty-five pounds overweight and wearing clothes that don't fit.

Not to mention, I couldn't find my contacts. Since I couldn't very well afford to go in blind, not tonight, not ever again, not with so much at stake, this meant wearing my glasses. They're not the cool kind, either. They're thick rimmed and pointy, the kind you buy when you're naive enough to think you already have a man and no one else's opinion matters. Let that be a lesson.

Speaking of lessons…not only is my hair and eyewear lacking, I clearly missed the memo about dressing up. My dark jeans and sweater are boring and plain in comparison to these women. Not unlike the rest of my life.

When Ethan said I let myself go, he wasn't being intentionally cruel. He just didn't know what it felt like to eat real food. He didn't know, not until after we were married, how tight a lid I kept on the *real* me and how life might look if I let it slip. Still, the weight and my appearance are not what made me lose my husband. But they certainly didn't help.

Now that he has one foot out the door, or rather both of them, if I'm honest, they aren't helping me get a job either. And I desperately need a job. They say appearance doesn't matter. But it so obviously does. As my husband said once, who in their right mind would trust you to handle their business if you can't even take care of yourself? Ann says your outer appearance is just a reflection of how you feel about yourself on the inside. Her critics eat her alive for it. They call her a fat-shamer. But even I have to admit, she isn't entirely wrong.

I used to be fit. In shape. On top of things. But that seems like ages ago. I was a different person then. I am not that person anymore.

I never imagined I'd be in this situation, although in hindsight, I really should have. It's fascinating the kind of damage people can do to themselves. It sort of just sneaks up on you. You think you know how low you can go, but really, there's always another level, another rock bottom.

This is the way it is, Ann says in her book. And then you die. You just sink lower and lower until the bitter end. Basically, it's like you're digging your own grave with all your bad decisions. Decisions can be different, she wants you to know. Things either get better or they don't, and then some part of your body gives— maybe it's your heart or your lungs or a combination of the two—

and then you die. It doesn't have to be this way, Ann says. But usually it is.

Ann says a lot of things. She believes in survival of the fittest, and she wants everyone else to believe in it too. But there are too many stupid people in this world for me to embrace that notion wholeheartedly.

Anyway, I need a job, and I don't have a job. And when you don't have a job your mind takes you places. Dark places.

My mind has hung out in those dark places for a while. Ethan hadn't wanted me to work. Initially, I'd been fine with that. But that was when life was full of promise for what lay ahead. That was when I had someone else's income to count on. I hadn't even missed much about my career at first, except for the connections. But then, I landed here at this dinner party and now I can see, I should have been more patient. Everything has a solution.

People mingle. People drink. People consume. No one speaks to me with any depth—but why would they? We have little in common. They've come for a party, and I am the opposite of that, too solid a reminder of what they might become if they aren't careful. Run down. Overweight. Alone.

No one wants a mirror held up to the fact that they, too, can slip, that things and people can be taken away without notice, simply because they can.

That's not to say the neighbors are unkind, even if they refuse to meet my eye. Probably most of them don't even notice me. Probably, like Ethan says, I am imagining things.

It doesn't feel like I'm imagining things. And anyway, like Ann writes in her book, feelings can be deceptive.

I have to give Ethan credit for being right about something. If I look closely, I can see he has a point. These people, they aren't thinking about me. They're all busy trying too hard. Most of the women here rarely get this dressed up on a weeknight. Even a Friday. There's not much to do in this town, and it's obvious they are eager, overly so, for the chance to feel seen.

I almost feel sorry for them. I want to text Ethan and let him know I understand now. It was all in my head. I want to make jokes, with our eyes from across the room, the way we used to. I want to feel his hand on the small of my back, his fingers intertwined with mine. I want to feel my back against the wall, my hair wound tightly in his fist. I wouldn't even mind his hand around my throat, suffocating me in the way only he could.

Mostly, I want to be eager to leave, eager to be alone together, eager to see the night end. But the night goes on forever and it never ends.

I'd like to tell him he had been right about other things, too—things I am now seeing in his absence. I want to tell him you can see a lot if you look closely enough. But I can't. Not yet.

CHAPTER SEVEN

SADIE

If you can't beat 'em, you might as well join them. In her book, Ann suggests that if I can change—if I can lose the weight, make friends—my life can be okay again. Not like before. Different. If I give it my best shot, if I try hard enough, things can be even better. Impossible, if you ask me. But to Ann, nothing is impossible.

I hope she isn't wrong, because I don't have long to figure it out. Currently, I have fourteen months of saved income left, minus what the cat is costing me. If I look on the bright side— the way Ann tells you in her book—it is still well above what the average American has in savings.

Unfortunately, this town isn't exactly cheap.

Ethan always wanted a big house, in a nice neighborhood, and back then, so did I. Back then, I hadn't budgeted for living in it all alone.

But I can't dwell on that. Not now.

Now, I have to do what Ann says and become the change I want to see. I'm getting a head start by standing at the Bankses' bookshelves, scanning their selection, when out of the corner of my eye, movement catches my attention. A teenage girl comes bounding down the stairs. It is obvious right away she is Ann's daughter. The striking eyes combined with the same friendly smile give her away. They're almost the same person. I watch as the girl surveys the crowd, clearly searching for someone. Unlike her mother, she hasn't yet learned to hide the things she doesn't want others to see.

She scans the room until finally her eyes land on me. They settle on the book in my hands. She takes the last of the steps two at a time, smiling wryly. "It's my mother's favorite," she tells me, moving in close. Her fingers brush the spine. She lowers her voice. "Better not let her see you touch it. She's known to remove fingers for lesser offenses."

I place the novel back on the shelf. Although, not before committing the title to heart. *House of Leaves.* "I'll keep that in mind."

"Have you seen my brother?" she asks. She poses the question as though I know who she is talking about, as though we aren't strangers, as though her parents know everyone and anyone there, thereby entitling her to the same. It reminds me what it was like to be her age. Sixteen or so, I presume. Oh, to have the world at your feet—to have the pleasure of being too dumb to know all of the mistakes you'll make and too smart to make all the ones you should.

"I haven't," I say. In fact, I haven't yet met Neil, the Bankses' oldest child, although in retrospect it was obvious he'd be home. He isn't the type to make friends easily, and in any case, Ann would want him around to show off.

A caterer swings by with a tray. I take an hors d'oeuvre and stuff it in my mouth. I find it interesting… at the grocery store, Ann spoke as though she were handling everything on her own. She made it sound like she was just having a few friends over for dinner—not the entirety of the neighborhood. Ann, ever the minimizer. Always one to under promise and over deliver. She posts that quote religiously on Instalook.

I have to give credit where credit is due. She certainly practices what she preaches. The music is just right. The lighting is great. Conversation flows. People enjoy themselves. In fact, every person I encounter emits the same sentiment. They can't believe their luck to have landed in the vicinity of such greatness. They don't say this outright, obviously. But it's there, under the surface, in their every comment about how wonderful the Bankses are, what an outstanding entertainer Ann is, how lovely the party has turned out.

The next time the caterer swings by with a tray, I grab a few extra hors d'oeuvres so I have reserves. I even make it a point to chew slowly. Not only can I savor the taste, but so long as I have food in my mouth, I don't have to actually speak to anyone. Food is comforting that way.

"Sadie!" Ann calls from the stairs. "You came."

"I can't stay for dinner," I say sorrowfully, in the way that I've practiced. "But I didn't want to be rude." I offer up the bottle of wine I brought. It's cheap on purpose, because I don't have a job but also, I want her to know how much I need her. And I really, really need her.

She takes the bottle from my hands and turns it over in hers. Not even a twitch, not a muscle moves in her face, and it isn't the Botox. She's *that* good at controlling her emotions. I want to be, too. "Oh, Sadie. You could never be rude."

Clearly, we aren't that well acquainted yet. Her response surprises me. I understand she is a trained liar, sure. I just thought I would see it coming, is all. Apparently, there aren't warning signs. I didn't know it was possible a person could radiate such warmth while lying to your face.

This leads me to believe that maybe there's more I don't know. Maybe with enough effort, I can come to understand the kind of stuff she is made of. Maybe then, I'll understand what's inside me. Maybe then, I'll know how far I, too, can go.

She motions me with her finger. "Would you mind helping me retrieve a few things from the garage?"

"Sure," I say, too eagerly. First lesson, all the nicety in the world can't make a person love you—and isn't that what we're all looking for to some degree? I know this so I follow as she leads the way.

"I almost forgot about the cheese tray…" Ann explains that she keeps everything out in the garage. *Out of sight, out of mind.* Her garage is detached from the house and she apologizes for the trek. She says at least it'll give us a chance to get to know each other, in peace. But she walks with purpose, leaving little time for small talk, and anyway by the time we reach the garage I'm out of breath. I try to hide how out of shape I am, but it's pretty obvious in my monosyllabic responses. Nerves cause me to be unsure of what to do with my hands so I stuff them in my pockets. Ann Banks has just said she wants to get to know me. If only, Ethan could see me now.

Ann opens the door to a subzero refrigerator before turning to me. It's dark and chilly and the lighting is poor. "You shouldn't stand like that," she says. "With your hands in your pockets. No one will trust you."

"Oh." I slip my hands from my pockets and blow into them, hoping it will warm me.

She peers into the freezer. "Body language is everything, Sadie."

My eyes search the garage, and as they adjust to the darkness, I spot a second refrigerator. "Would you mind grabbing the half and half?" She points noticing where my attention has gone. "It's in that one."

"Your home is lovely," I remark, once I've done as she's asked.

She sighs wistfully. "Our last house was much bigger."

"You must miss it."

"We lost everything," she tells me. "Well, almost everything"—

she slams the refrigerator door— "okay—not almost everything. But a lot."

"I'm sorry—"

"We still have each other, and that's what counts."

"Exactly," I say, because truer words have never been spoken. I'm beginning to think Ann's followers are onto something. More than anything, I want to find out what her perceived losses are. She tells me about Stan at the grocery store, and how she heard that he hadn't pulled through after all. Something about a brain bleed from his fall. *Such a terrible thing,* she says. *Such a waste.* She doesn't say whether it was Creepy Stan or her efforts that were wasted but I get the sense she means the latter.

"Have you ever felt like killing someone Sadie?"

At first, I think I've heard her wrong. Her voice conveyed little emotion, so it's hard to tell. When I turn to face her, she is calm and composed. But it's clear she's awaiting an answer.

"No."

"Never?"

I shake my head. "I don't think so."

"Well, I have. Darcy White. Do you know Darcy?"

I shake my head again. Ann talks very fast. It's like listening to an audiobook on triple speed. Ethan used to do that. Hearing is the fastest sense, he'd say if I complained. The human body can hear faster than it can see, taste, smell, or feel. Once a sound wave reaches your ear, your brain can recognize it in just 0.05 seconds, something he seemed to like to test.

"Darcy," Ann says. "She recommended this caterer, and something deep down said I shouldn't listen. Alarm bells went off. Clear as day. I knew I shouldn't have hired her. I knew it. If I didn't need her to like me for the sake of my kids…her children carry a lot of weight at school I hear…you know… I might have listened. But I didn't listen—and now I have dozens of overcooked appetizers on my hands."

I leaned forward with enthusiasm. I could fix this in a jiffy, but

I'd probably better not. Ethan always said, less is more. I just hadn't realized he'd actually meant it.

When I fail to offer a response, Ann apprises me carefully. "What is one supposed to do with a situation like this?"

I note the way she poses a question—what she doesn't say is what *she* plans to do about it. In fact, I'm surprised she brought up Darcy White. I doubted she'd go for the ones on a level playing field.

"I'm sure it will be fine," I offer, which is exactly the wrong thing to say. I realize this when she corners me.

"IT WILL NOT BE FINE."

I stare at her in that wild-eyed and languid way one does when they aren't sure what to say. Ann is tall and scary. I am short and lumpy. Sure, I could probably take her on size alone, but I'm sure she's accounted for that. Now, there's nothing but cheese and cold half and half between us and no way out of this. She's staring me down. She's waiting for something to happen, for me to say something, for me to show fear.

I feel nothing.

Well, I feel something. But I don't think it's fear. I'd say it's more along the lines of a rush. Something close to excitement. Something I can't put my finger on. Something I haven't felt in a long time.

"Did you know fear can be a turn on, Sadie?"

"I didn't," I say. But I'm moved by her display of emotion. I realize she and I are one and the same. If the lid is kept on for too long, eventually it slips. Her rage is like a fast car: zero to sixty in no time. Maybe she senses this, and maybe this is why she steps off the gas. "Don't be ridiculous," she says, and just like that she slams the brake. She retreats backward. She smooths her dress. "No one likes dry chicken, Sadie. We have to get rid of them."

"The caterers?"

Ann gives me the side eye. "No, the appetizers. My husband

will kill me if he finds out I threw them away. Paul hates waste of any kind."

"What should we do with them?"

"Do you know about the three Ps?"

I don't, but I make a mental note to learn them quickly. "I could hide them in my car."

"Perfect," she says with a curt nod. "Do that."

I realize it was a dumb thing to say, in retrospect. No one wants to drive around smelling like chicken salad tarts, and yet I bet that's exactly what Ann wanted to happen. Clearly, this was a test. The first of many. I wasn't sure I'd passed. Something just told me I wanted to.

CHAPTER EIGHT

HER

The weight of the gas pedal feels good beneath my foot. Driving a car with this kind of power gives me the third best kind of rush, just below fucking and killing.

Maybe I shouldn't drive so fast. Maybe I don't know these roads like I think I do. But as Julia Roberts says in *Pretty Woman*, this car corners like it's on rails, and if I wasn't enjoying the feel of it so much I might ease up a bit.

But I don't.

Which is why it's a beautiful day that's about to be ruined in 3...2...1. *Fuck. Fuck. Fuck.* One second everything is fine, and the next someone is flying through the air. Gravity being what it is, well—what goes up must come down. On the descent it's clear what's happened.

A lady.

On a bike.

A car going too fast.

Bright sunlight.

Terrible timing.

The woman hits the pavement like a rubber ball, bouncing a

few times then rolling before coming to a full stop in the brush. *What goes up, must come down.*

The scene is awful. I don't think I've ever seen a human leg twisted that way. If I were *her,* and I had a weaker stomach, I might have lost my lunch too. But, no. I have to be strong. Vomit is evidence, and there's no sense in leaving any of that behind.

Upon closer inspection, the way the woman is splayed out in the dirt, in the weeds, in the thick of it, is really quite beautiful. She isn't conscious. Speed was a factor. Regardless, in her condition, it's doubtful she'll make it long anyhow. Aside, from the obvious broken bones, most of her damage will be internal. *So as in life, as it is in death.*

I want to feel bad for her. But I don't. She ruined what was meant to be a beautiful day. It's really too bad people use bicycles in places meant for cars. There's too much room for error, and clearly one person has the advantage. Thankfully for me, it wasn't the cyclist. Wish I could say the same for the car.

CHAPTER NINE

SADIE

A lot happened between Ann and I after I did her a solid by hiding the appetizers in my car. I guess you could say things moved quickly. From that evening on, Ann began texting me incessantly.

I didn't mind. It's so much easier to cultivate a relationship when you have time to curate the perfect response. You hardly even have to be yourself. You just write what you think the other person wants to hear.

But, if she wasn't texting, she was calling. She'd hang up, think of something else, and call right back. Sometimes I didn't answer just so she'd text instead and I could savor her words like they belonged to me. Because, to my mind, they did. I was learning her language. I was learning to speak like she spoke. I made her feel understood. That's how we became what you call fast friends.

But not too fast. I didn't see her mow the caterer over with her car with my own two eyes, but I know she did it. She was smart about it. A quiet farm-to-market road. Bright sunny day. Zero witnesses. Cyclists are hit all the time, I overheard her say to a neighbor.

Turns out, Ann's caterer was an avid cyclist. The odds were

against her, Ann said. Four deaths in Driftwood, just this year alone. The woman was in the wrong place at the wrong time, Ann said. Sure, she made poor decisions that led to her fate. She was lucky, Ann told me. She died doing what she loved. Not all of us get that kind of good fortune. The sad part, I concluded, was she probably didn't even get the message.

But I did.

For several days after the accident, Ann kept to herself. At the time, I chalked it up to the impending holidays. Later, I'd learn this was her style. After hosting one of her parties, she liked to take a step back. She'd go really big and then she'd sit back and let her prey come to her.

Thankfully, I was busy. Ann had surprised me by pulling some major strings. Thanks to her, I got a job as a substitute at the local high school. Most of the regular subs like to take time off to prepare for the holidays, and teachers are prone to want to do the same, she told me before I had the chance to mention that I hate children. Teenagers especially.

Unfortunately, my bank account couldn't care less.

At this point, work equals keeping my head above water. I either kill what I eat or I don't eat. Had it not been for Ann's recommendation, I don't think the school would have called, so I can't help but feel grateful. Given my history, I'm not even sure how she pulled it off, other than the administration is known to enjoy her parties too. Well, there's that—and there's her growing fame.

It pays to be an internet celebrity. An influencer, they call them, and let me tell you, I for one am glad for that. Influence is important, Ann says.

She isn't wrong about that. Clearly, she's aware of what's happening in the world. She understands the system and she's prepared. I know I need to be too. You used to be able to escape your past buried in high school yearbooks or local papers, but today in the digital age, you are judged from cradle to grave. Big

Tech sifts, sorts, and sells all your data to the highest bidder whether that be business or governments. In China, social scoring is used for pretty much everything. Citizens are issued social credit scores based on how trustworthy or credible they are perceived to be. Their behaviors are tracked and traced, and they're ranked on these things by algorithms. Like the domino effect, it trickles down until they just start shutting down your life, one keystroke at a time. A few wrong moves and your access to things like public transportation is denied and your bank account is revoked. This system is coming to the States—I can feel it. It's already happening online. It's like boiling a frog or whatever. Even now, if you're a model, or an actress, or a musician, unless you have a certain number of social media followers, it's nearly impossible to get a gig.

Long story long, my credibility is lacking. Ann was kind enough to let me borrow hers. Obviously, this can't last forever, which is unfortunate. The thing that happened last year doesn't help. While the incident didn't involve children, Driftwood is a small town, and people talk. Needless to say, my social credit took a hit.

Now, the time has come to rebuild. I only wish someone had told me that making friends as an adult isn't any easier than it is as a kid. It's worse. You have all of those hardened beliefs and insecurities to contend with. And those at the top? They like to stay there.

At least I have a job. The people there don't have a choice about being my friend. We're destined to spend time together. Even if substituting is pretty much the last thing on the planet I had in mind when it came to employment, I'll make it work. Besides, this isn't the city. There aren't a ton of options for work out here. Driving into Austin wouldn't kill me, but the anxiety might.

Thankfully, subbing does come with at least one perk aside from the paycheck—tiny as it may be—it gives me the opportunity to observe the Bankses' children. Being in such close proximity, you learn a lot. Already, I know Amelia is like her mom, dazzling. Neil is also like his mother, dark and brooding, but also quiet and reverent. It is interesting to see how these things can exist in one person simultaneously. I'm beginning to wonder if they might exist in me too.

Ann says in her book that life is about the journey. I realize that this gig, this friendship, is an opportunity for a fresh start. If I'm careful, if I play my cards right, it can be a new beginning for me.

Sure, I have reservations. Especially when I consider Ann plowing down that woman on her bike. Strangely, I can empathize with her frustration at the level of incompetence over the appetizers. Little things are important when your reputation is on the line. Believe me, I know. And in any case, now it feels like we have a secret.

That's not to say I think the punishment fit the crime.

I'm not a monster.

I have my moments where I waffle back and forth about what to do about my suspicions. *Should I go to the police?* Maybe. *Should I tell someone?* Probably. But it's not like my track record is all together squeaky-clean. Besides, I didn't actually see it happen, and you can't very well ruin someone's life on a hunch. The last thing I need is cops asking questions—or worse— pointing fingers. Not now that I finally have a job and a friend.

A lot is riding on this and I'm counting on Ann. She is helping me—even if she doesn't yet understand to what extent. With any luck, I can improve my social standing, and maybe even get my husband back. Maybe there is still a chance that what she says in her book, about my life getting better, could be true.

And who knows?

Maybe it was an accident, even if it didn't sound like one.

CHAPTER TEN

SADIE

The chairs are lined in rows, not in a circle like I pictured in my mind. This bothers me more than I let on. In her chart topping motivational book, Ann says we have to let go of expectations. Believe me, this is harder than she makes it sound. Here, we don't hold hands, and no one feels sorry for anyone, not really. We've all come for the same reason and mostly not by choice. It's court ordered. I suppose this explains why no one is particularly friendly or happy to be here.

Here, they aren't concerned with social scores or social standings. They don't seem to be aware of what's happening in the world. Or perhaps maybe they are, and that's what landed them here. In an attempt to find out what I'm working with, I strike up a conversation with a short odd looking woman who is seated next to me. "Do you know what's happening?" I whisper.

"Well, sweetheart, I hate to break it to you," she answers a little too loudly for my liking. "But they aren't handing out awards, if that's what you're thinkin'."

I tell her about the social credit score.

Her eyes narrow. "What're you talking about? Social credit?"

"Companies are basing our car insurance rates, our interest

rates, on what we do on the internet. They're cataloging every digital move we make."

I expect her to be outraged, or at the very least surprised. But she isn't. Instead, she cocks her head and looks at me like I'm the crazy one, when she's the one with electric blue hair and more piercings than I can accurately count in a thirty second conversation. "Honey," she says. "Ain't no one here got any kinda good credit anyway."

I consider telling her more. I consider warning her about what's coming down the pipeline, about the need to take this seriously. But she scoffed at me, and I hate a scoffer. Anyway, it's no use. Like my husband, she doesn't want to hear it either. I settle into my seat and prepare myself for the long haul.

These meetings are the same every time or at least the three times I have attended in the past week. We meet, we state our names, and then we are educated on the dangers of drugs and alcohol and the perils of living under the influence.

I'm not like these people. I'm not an addict. I made a mistake. A simple mistake. A rookie mistake. In fact, I'm so new at this I thought I could serve my time by just showing up. I thought the more meetings I attended, the better off I'd be. I thought it'd earn me brownie points. I thought I'd be pardoned on good behavior. But that's a different kind of system, the instructor said. Not this one.

It's fine, I told him. Aside from trying to earn a living, it's not like I have anything else to do.

He says knowing we aren't alone is good practice for getting out in the world again. He says sometimes our demons can feel real but they aren't, and that it's up to us to fight them.

He's partly right. The class requires me to drive into Austin for this, which means I have to take an Ativan at least thirty minutes prior to getting in the car.

On the way, I stopped and bought a coffee, the most expensive latte I could afford. Even though I can't really afford a six dollar cup of something I could make on my own for next to nothing. The coffee makes me feel accomplished. It makes me feel like my demons can't get the best of me, not so long as I stay one step ahead. It makes me feel normal, not like I have to pop a pill just to get in my car and drive somewhere. It almost makes me forget that if I don't do something, and fast, I'm never going to get a real job, or a decent interest rate, or have friends or a family of my own. Those are normal people things, and that pill is a reminder. I am not normal. If it costs me six bucks to fool myself, then so be it. Ann says this is impossible. She says people can't lie to themselves as easily as they think they can. But she can't see me here with my fancy cup. She can't see how put-together I look. Not like the rest of them.

I'm different. I look like I shouldn't be here, like I actually care to make my life better. And I do. I sit in the front row and sip my poison-flavored latte slowly and righteously, just to prove my point.

Ethan showed me the ingredients once. It's absolute garbage, he'd said. What you're putting into your body and the amount of money you're spending to ingest toxins, he ranted, was reprehensible.

We all die some way, I assured him. *At least my death won't come cheap, and it'll taste good.* He didn't laugh like he might have once. I feel like I don't even know who you are, he told me, and that was the day I learned: marriages have social scores too.

The lady beside me scoffs again. I don't take it personally. I don't think she likes the speaker. It's fine. I realize this probably isn't the kind of place I want to be making friends anyhow. I don't know if *some* are better than *none*, but probably not. Still, I learn their names anyway. Just in case. There's a guy named Keith, whose eyes make me think of the Grand Canyon. Cassidy, young and pretty, who couldn't care less. James, who cries.

I like it here. The rest, I forget.

I forget because Ann texts and asks if I'd like to come down for coffee later that afternoon. I'm relieved. It'll be nice to see her. If only she'd asked earlier, back when I was six dollars richer.

Sometimes I like to think about reversing time, about what it would be like if you could hit a rewind button, if we could get do-overs. Ann says in her book that there's no point in looking back, that we can only move forward.

I decide to test her theory by saying yes to coffee at her place. It's not like I have anything else particularly interesting to do.

There is only one not-so-tiny little problem. I learned something this morning that I think Ann would want to know. Something that will cut to the core. It's unfortunate, finding out something you can't un-know. Already, I realize what an issue this is going to be if our friendship is to continue. Things are not as perfect in Ann's world as she would like to believe. I just don't want to be the one to have to tell her.

I know I'm supposed to be trustworthy. But am I trustworthy enough to break her heart? I haven't yet decided. For one, I don't want to mess up a good thing.

It's a perverse choice. But I can't tell her. Not yet. You can't deliver news like that and remain on a person's good side. Anyway, who says you have to be honest about *everything*? Omission isn't exactly lying. Besides, timing is important. I know this better than anyone.

Coffee can't hurt though, can it? It's not like she's a mind reader. Just in case, I make it a point to push what I've learned from my memory like my social worker taught me to do after my mother's death.

I practice by spending the rest of DUI class thinking about getting a dog and which breed might be most suitable. Something small might be nice, but something big and protective could work too. It is a nice fantasy while it lasts. When I mention it to the lady with the blue hair, she gives me that look again and tells me dogs are like children, just another thing to possibly fuck up.

CHAPTER ELEVEN

SADIE

I t helps to know what kind of moral gray area you're dealing with, Ann says. She picked me up in my driveway and said we should go out for coffee instead. She said she needed to get away from Penny Lane and wondered if I might want to come along. She suggested we do something crazy, something to take her mind off of things.

Ann has a way of making seemingly small things like coffee feel like a grand adventure, so, of course, I knew I wanted in.

Now, she is sitting behind the wheel staring at her phone. "This will only take a minute," she tells me as her fingers furiously text away.

It's nothing new. That's what I've learned about her. Ann always seems to be working. She always has an angle.

"There," she says, finally. "Now that *that's* done, let's get coffee."

"Then what?"

"Then we wait."

I don't know what we're waiting for. But Ann seems happy, and she isn't thinking about overcooked appetizers or work, or hit and runs or overly emotional teenagers, or any of the stuff she said on the way here is nonsense, and that is kind of nice. It's hard to get her to open up when she's in one of her moods. She shores it up, battens down the hatches, tightens her borders.

After we place our order at the drive thru, and Ann pays for our coffees—she insists—she parks in the lot. She didn't elaborate on what exactly she meant by "do something crazy," but maybe in her world, a chai latte in the afternoon qualifies. Maybe this is the skinny people's version of letting loose.

I wouldn't know.

We don't talk much; we do what Ann tells me is her favorite hobby: we people watch. She says it's why she went into her field. Which makes sense. She tells me she's glad we met. She needs a friend she can be perfectly comfortable in silence with. It's rare, she assures me. She says most people can't shut up long enough to actually have a thought, and I can't help but smile. It's nice to have finally found something precious and rare.

The silence doesn't last long, because Ann's phone rings. She doesn't answer with a hello nor does she offer pleasantries. She asks how she can help. There are no take-backs on this, she says calmly into the receiver. I listen as she coaxes the caller's address. She teases it out, choosing her words carefully before finally letting out a long sigh. "This is your third call this week. At some point, Kelsey, you have to ask yourself if you're really serious—if you really have it within you to go through with it at all."

I can't hear the other end of the conversation, obviously. "Remember," Ann says before hanging up, her face impassive, "death is final."

After she ends the call she looks over at me and apologizes. Ann tells me about the suicide hotline she operates. It's a very busy time of year—the busiest, she says—on account of the holidays and the weather. Sometimes when they are short on volunteers, she has to forward the calls to her cell phone. The alternative, she says, is people die.

⁓

"I BET THAT'S HER," ANN EXCLAIMS, PEERING OVER THE RIM OF HER cup, which is interesting because I hadn't realized we were waiting on anyone. There's a part of me that is disappointed. I was under the impression we were sitting in the car because Ann says it is more private that way. You never know who is listening, she says. She's sick of taking selfies. She likes her privacy. And, she can't leave the hotline unmanned for too long.

"Here." When I look over, she is forcing a switchblade in my direction.

"What's this?"

Ann points to a tall woman wearing a skirt with boots and a ponytail. "You see that BMW she got out of?"

"Yeah."

"I want you to stab her."

"What?"

She laughs. "I'm kidding. You don't have to stab her." Her eyes search mine. "Well, not unless you want to."

"Yeah, no. I don't."

"Fine," she sighs. "Go for the rear tires instead."

"I can't do that," I declare vigorously. "It's illegal."

"Could you if that woman were fucking your husband?"

"No," I tell her, but then I picture Ethan with someone else and I'm forced to admit, "I don't know."

"You do know, Sadie. You do." Ann motions with the nod of her head. "Now don't dilly-dally—she won't be in there long—trust me, as soon as she finds out there's no one waiting for her, she'll be out the door."

"Ann, I can't."

"You know...I get calls every day—multiple times a day—from women just like Kelsey. Lives are destroyed by women just like that one, Sadie. Kelsey wants to die but part of her already has. Sometimes," she says, "It's all we can do to even the score."

I take a deep breath in and mull over what she's just said. "I'm sorry," I tell her. "I can't."

Ann studies my face very carefully. Then she does that thing with her eyes she does when she gets angry. "Fine," she tells me before she snatches the knife from my hand, very deftly I might add, like she's practiced at it. "I want you to listen, Sadie," she says. "Are you listening?"

The blade glistens in the sunlight. I'm all ears.

"I want you to hop in the driver's seat, put the car in gear, and watch me."

And watch her, I do. I've never seen anything so efficient in all my life. Sweat beads at my hairline. My heart races. My throat goes dry. I forget to breathe, until I realize I might be suffocating. I've never felt so alive.

I expect that people will notice what Ann is doing. The coffee shop is a busy place.

I am wrong. Everyone is too busy staring at their phones, too preoccupied with feeding their afternoon addictions, to notice what is happening right under their nose.

She goes around to the passenger side of the woman's car. I'm thinking, *who will believe me that this happened? Maybe we are going to jail. Maybe we are Thelma and Louise.* We are not Thelma and Louise. The coffee shop probably has cameras. Everyone does these days. *I'm an accomplice.*

I don't even notice I'm digging my nails into my palm, not until I see Ann walking briskly back to the car. She opens the passenger door and climbs in and orders me to drive.

When I'm pretty sure we're in the clear, I ask if she does this often.

"Only when I need to feel something."

I wait for her to expand on that but she doesn't. She tells me to hold my thoughts. She has to text the woman with the boots.

"This, Sadie," she says, "This is one way to know you're alive."

I wonder what other ways there might be.

"God!" she exclaims as she brushes her bangs out of her eyes. "Doesn't it feel good?"

It does feel good, I admit. Watching Ann do the kind of terrible things I thought she might be capable of feels very good indeed. It feels like the kind of rush I haven't felt in a very long time. "Who was she?"

She shrugs. "Hell if I know." Her voice is expressive, almost giddy. The exasperation from earlier is gone. "Sometimes I just like to pretend I'm someone else," she says. "You know?"

I don't think I do. But I'm learning.

"I found her on one of those dating apps that married people use to get some on the side. We've been chatting for two days now. You should see the stuff she told me, Sadie. You wouldn't believe it."

When I look over, Ann is staring at her phone. She glances up and laughs. "I just texted her my apologies. Told her I got caught up at work."

I wait for her to offer more. But the next time I look over, she is staring straight ahead, smiling manically. "God, Sadie. Some people are so gullible. Bet you anything she was planning our future—and we hadn't even met. That's how desperate people are. They'll believe anything you tell them. She thought I was a plumber named Rob. I wasn't even original—I didn't have to be. I mean...how boring is that? You can just say whatever...it's literally *that* easy."

Plumbing is actually a very intricate profession. But I don't think Ann wants to hear this.

"Oh, and Sadie," she says, as she adjusts her seatbelt, "I'm investing a lot of emotional energy in you—in this friendship." She motions between the two of us. "It's important you understand—I'm very careful about who I spend time with. Back there, that was your one free pass. If you can't hang," she tells me, "You can't hang. Better I know sooner rather than later."

CHAPTER TWELVE

SADIE

On the drive home, Ann wants me to tell her about my childhood. This isn't all that surprising; she's a therapist, and they always start there. I've always felt it's sort of a waste of time. Life is in the now. The past is the past. Ann says I'm right. But she says self-awareness is important. History has a way of repeating itself.

She couldn't be less wrong about that. We pass the gym, and she goes on talking about psychology and overcoming trauma. But I'm not listening. I'm too busy living it. The gym reminds me of the final straw before the final straw with Ethan. It came only days after that perfect day on the beach where my husband and I kept our eyes on the sky, where he tethered me to the earth.

"I'm starting yoga soon," I say to Ann. It's not the truth. But it could be. I want her to know I can hang. I want her to know that she is right to invest what she calls "emotional energy" on me.

"Yoga is amazing."

I smile because Ethan thought that too. He'd gifted me the gym membership. Someone at his office was into yoga, and he thought I ought to be too. It was just a suggestion, he said, when I was less than thrilled. But it was more than that. The gym was a simple gift that wasn't a gift at all. It was a sign.

It was a sign that he wanted to take the little game we had been playing to the next level. And I was livid. He couldn't understand why.

So I shifted my strategy. I figured two could play at his game. After all, why use words to get your point across when you can just as easily do it passive aggressively, disguised as a gift?

It's not like I didn't know he wanted me to lose the weight. He didn't have to say it with words or with a gym membership. I knew he wanted me to stop being depressed, as though it were that simple. I knew he wanted me to find something that fulfilled me.

Just not a job, apparently.

Ethan said he wanted me to be happy. But what he really wanted was to have me around to meet his needs.

That's what a wife is supposed to do, after all.

I'm still not exactly sure what a husband is supposed to do.

Suggest quick fixes, I suppose.

Part of strategy was giving him the silent treatment, his least favorite form of punishment. For days, he apologized profusely. He hadn't meant for the gym membership to be such a big deal. He tried to make up with sex. As usual, finally, in the end, we played by his rules. As usual, it was over before it started.

It wasn't until later, after we lay on the couch, my head on his chest, that I realized maybe he was right. Maybe there was no reason to be so unhappy. Maybe it was time to take things to the next level. After all, most women would kill for the kind of life I have. Ethan might have said that once or twice. I know my mother would have. And now, here I am with Ann, and she's asking about her. Talk about coming full circle.

"If you want to understand the relationships in your life," she says, "You have to start with your parents…"

"I hardly knew them. My mother worked three jobs."

"And your father?"

"Hardly worked at all. But he wasn't around much."

"What did your mother do for a living?"

"She owned a cleaning business—very successful," I say. It isn't totally a lie. I leave a few things out.

During the week my mother cleaned houses. She washed other people's dishes, handled other people's dirty laundry. It was her own she didn't handle so well.

"What about weekends? What did you do for fun, growing up?"

Fun wasn't really in my vocabulary as a child. "I read."

"Ah, so you were a bit like me."

No, I was nothing like you. "The classics were my favorite. I suppose because they were easy to come by."

"It must have been hard being raised by a single mom."

You have no idea. "Not really. She was a hard worker. She did the best she could," I tell her. She seems satisfied because none of it is lies. On weekends my mother worked at a dry cleaners. Whatever it took, she said, to keep a roof over our heads. But weeknights were different. Weeknights were all hers, so to speak. That's when I was to make myself scarce. That's when she entertained men. Serving others with household matters offered up a steady clientele at our doorstep. My mother worked herself to death, but I don't think it was the work that killed her.

"She died when you were young?"

My fingers loosen on the steering wheel. "I was thirteen... how'd you know?"

"It's my job. You can usually tell. You have that air about you."

"Oh."

"How'd she die?"

"Cancer," I say, and this isn't exactly a lie either. My mother did have something eating at her. Something she was powerless to stop from growing. The first time she attempted to end things, I was five. I walked home from kindergarten to find her bleeding out on the bathroom floor.

She was sorry, she said days later when I visited her in the hospital. We didn't have family, and I assume as usual, my father was nowhere to be found. Thankfully, one of her housekeeping clients was kind enough to take me in.

Ann clears her throat. "Was it quick at least?"

"Not really."

At first, or rather that first time, it wasn't so bad. I got to sleep in her client's daughter's room while she was away at horse camp. Her bed wasn't a pallet on the floor like mine. She had a pink, frilly comforter and books. *So many books.* I could have any of them I wanted, her father said. They were relics, he told me. Classics, but also, his daughter only cared about boys.

"I'm sorry, Sadie," Ann says. "That must have been hard."

The second time was hard. I didn't get to go to the nice people's house. By then my mother had burned that bridge too. Nothing lasts forever, she'd said, when the woman got wise and fired her, and the books stopped coming. That time, I was eleven, and she hadn't slit her wrists. I was grateful that at least there wasn't the blood or the sight of her open flesh. That time, she sat in the garage with the car running. Only she ran out of gas before it killed her.

"It could have been worse," I say, glancing over at Ann. "She was brave. She died peacefully."

My mother was still sitting in the car by the time I'd trekked all the way home from school in the rain. She said she hadn't had enough gas to pick me up but we both knew it was a lie. She'd been weeping for days. She loved him, she swore. He discarded her. He used her, just like the rest of them. He'd never intended to leave his wife. I'd heard it all before. And so on it went.

"No, Sadie," Ann says taking my hand. "It was you who was brave."

I don't pull away, because her hand is soft and warm and she has a point.

For a while after the garage incident, I skipped school to go to work with my mother. In truth, I wanted to keep an eye on her in case she tried anything again. But there was the other issue as well. She was too sad to clean, and we desperately needed the money, so I did it for her. Thankfully, this only lasted a few weeks.

By then, she had a new client, and she was in love again.

The upswing lasted until I was thirteen.

That time, the car didn't run out of gas. It kept running, and it was still running when I arrived home.

Ann squeezes my hand. "So your father raised you then?"

"Something like that," I say, and she smiles. Me too, because she leaves it at that, which is better than having to tell the truth. I went straight into foster care. Four months and one black eye later, I disappeared into the night.

CHAPTER THIRTEEN

SADIE

Ann asks about my parents. But she forgets to ask about the most significant relationship of my life, which would make a lot more sense. If she is looking for insight as to who I am, she should have started there.

It wasn't long after the fight over my weight gain that Ethan started disappearing into the night too. Work was chaotic and stressful, he said. He began coming home later and later. There were major projects, he was climbing the ladder, and it was never quite the right time to slow down.

On weekends he started going to meet-ups with other people he said were interested in bettering themselves. He started mentoring youth through a program at work. He said it made him feel alive. He said he felt young again. Once or twice, he invited me to tag along. By that point, I had become just bitter enough not to take him up on the offer.

Instead, I busied myself by watching the neighbors. I guessed at their problems—at how many of them were just as unhappy and bored as I was. Sometimes I guessed right.

I told my husband about the woman next door that flew into

rages and hit her husband. I told him that the family down the street was hiding something. Something big. I learned who was having financial problems and who was relying on substances other than food, trashy TV, and voyeurism to get them through the day. I made it a point to share these things with Ethan just so he could see I wasn't really *that* bad.

Sure, we weren't as happy as we could be. And sure, we hardly spent any time together anymore. But isn't that what happens in a marriage? You settle in. The newlywed phase fades, and real life begins.

The truth is, I wasn't sure. I watched the neighbors to find out.

All the while, I continued reporting back to him. Until he started calling it my little obsession. He was playful about it at first. But once, I overheard him on the phone with his mother talking about "my little obsession" and I confronted him about it.

He said I was paranoid. He tossed out words like schizophrenia and obsessive compulsive disorder. He accused me of forgetting things, normal things, like grocery shopping and his mother's birthday. He accused me of not wanting to leave the house for fear I might miss something. That part, I'll admit was true. I hate his mother, and as for groceries, I figured what's the point, if only one of us is around to eat them?

But that night, the night that things got really bad, the night they took a turn for the worse, along with his accusations, he threw in an ultimatum. The final straw. Either I get happy—either I go to the gym—or we call it quits and go our separate ways.

I hadn't expected him to take such a strong stance. The truth is, I hadn't realized my appearance was that important to him. He said he hadn't realized it might become so unimportant to me. Before that night, I thought I had time. I thought everything would work itself out. I should have known better.

That was the night he gave me the book—Ann's book. He'd met her husband. They were renovating the house down the street. What are the odds, he wanted to know. How lucky we were, he said. He'd heard good things about the book from someone at his self-help meet-up. The book would help me, he said. No matter what happened between us, he said, he just wanted me to be happy. He said we could still be friends. He said it as though we were children, not grown people with a mortgage and plans for the future.

Suddenly, I was suffocating under the weight of his words. He was serious, I could see. Not only that—he'd just put a deadline on our relationship—on how I should behave, how I should think, on who I should be. The walls were closing in, and I'd just learned that the one good thing I had wanted to go away, too. Just like my career. Just like my father. Like my mother. Like everything.

He wanted to fix me. I wanted time.

I was naïve. I didn't have an exit strategy.

Clearly, he did.

My husband is a lot of things, but he is not a person who makes empty threats. When I told him I couldn't give him an answer on the spot, he tried to play his game and gifted me twenty-four hours.

All I could think in that moment was that I needed a drink or a hit of cocaine— something, anything—to take the edge off.

I had the feeling I'd landed myself in one of those choose-your-own-adventure books, the kind I adored as a kid. I always read both endings, even after I'd made my choice. In real life, that wasn't an option. You can't have it both ways. In real life, neither adventure seemed all that enticing.

I knew there wasn't any alcohol in the house, save for champagne, and that's not exactly the drink of choice when one is at the end of their marriage and their rope. So I grabbed my keys and stormed out. He thought I couldn't leave the house. Well, I'd show him.

To be clear, I'm not a drinker. It just sounded like something that might help in the moment.

It's not that I was oblivious to the fact that I should be able to give my husband what he wants. I practiced that form of magic my whole life. I can fake it, but eventually, even that gets old.

This was supposed to be easier. I love Ethan. I think he loves me. But when it isn't easy, it's hard. So I pretended everything was fine, when it so clearly wasn't. *Just give them what they want. Men are very simple.* Food, sex, and enough compliments to continuously stroke their ego. It's that easy. My mother used to say that. Housekeeping is a tough business, she told me. Her work, she believed, was keeping families together. You had to be careful about it. *You never want to make another woman feel inadequate, Sadie. Women are far smarter than we're given credit for.* Walk the tightrope, she used to say. Wave your white flag, if you have to. But keep your mouth shut and don't overstep your bounds.

I figured that's all I had to do when it came to marriage, too. Although, by the time I needed that kind of advice, my mother was long gone, and I was no longer sure I had it in me to be so compliant.

I worried that Ethan was right. That I'd lost my edge. In the old days, back in college, we used alcohol to solve fights. It was how we started them too. *Good ol' Stoli.*

I realized it probably wasn't the way to fix things anymore, not now that we were grown adults with real problems, the kind of problems the kids we were back then couldn't even fathom.

I wish my mother had warned me that love isn't enough. I wish she'd explained more in words than with her life that someday I, too, might want more and yet not even be able to put my finger on what that thing is.

I wish I had known that my husband would only desire me when I was thin(ish), when I was climbing the corporate ladder, when I was like him. I wish I had known that the reasons he fell in love with me would be the very things he'd set out to extinguish.

But I hadn't known, and liquor seemed like the next best thing to dealing with the truth. It was suddenly blatantly clear. Unless I did something bold. Unless I made a drastic course correction, it was over.

Where are you going, Ethan had texted me. He'd accused me of acting irrationally. He worried I'd do something stupid, something irreversible. He forgot one thing.

I'm not him.

I didn't respond. Not even when he called. I wanted to make him pay. I wanted him to understand what a bad decision he was making. I wanted him to see how out of control I could be. And if I couldn't succeed at any of that, at the very least, I wanted to fix it like we used to.

The pathetic part: I didn't even know where the closest liquor store was; I had to search on my phone.

Unfortunately, luck wasn't on my side when it came to being a good wife or fixing it when I was a bad one. In Texas, liquor stores close at 9:00 p.m. I made it to the register at 8:58.

Only it turned out the woman in front of me was paying for her hooch in nickels and dimes, shaming the rest of us for our purchases by mere chance.

By the time the clerk had finished counting, and I made it to the front of the line, it was 9:03. "I'm sorry," she said. "I can't sell you this."

I had my ID ready, just in case, and I presented it.

"No," she informed me. "If the register reads past nine p.m., I can't make the sale."

A man behind me groaned. He set his six-pack in the middle of the floor and walked out.

I thanked the woman before returning the bottle to the shelf. I picked up the man's beer and handed it to the cashier. "There's a bar down the street," she offered with a smile.

And that's where I ended up.

Two vodka cherry sours is all it took.

Flashing lights behind me. I hadn't swerved. I hadn't sped. I hadn't even *felt* drunk.

It was the taillight I had been after Ethan to fix.

CHAPTER FOURTEEN

SADIE

The way Ann watches me come up the lane makes me feel uneasy. The Ativan I popped helps to take the edge off, but it doesn't make the anxiety go away altogether. *Does she know where I've been? Does she know about my misdeeds? Does she know what I'm keeping from her?* Ann has a way of looking straight through you, and even I know that's easier to do at a distance. She asked me to come down for coffee. And, because there's something she wants to show me.

"Do you think it's too much?" she asks when I reach the porch.

I have no idea what she's talking about. I don't want to seem stupid which forces me to wait for her to explain. Finally, she motions toward the yard.

In the daylight, and in wondering if she thinks I am capable of prison time, if I am good enough to have coffee with, worthy of being her friend, of keeping a small animal alive, I hadn't noticed the Christmas decorations.

I realize I shouldn't care so much about what anyone else thinks. But I do. I really, really do. My plan can't work if I don't.

Idle hands. Ethan never should have suggested I leave my job. If I hadn't, I wouldn't have had time to read so many internet articles or watch 24/7 newsfeeds about the destruction of everything we know, our planet included. How can you escape from that? Because if America goes the way of China and implements an official social credit score—I don't want to be screwed.

Trust me. You can't. Destruction is inevitable. You hear about addictions all the time. I thought addictions were about things that made you feel good. Or at the very least, made you feel nothing at all. No one warns you that you can become addicted to knowing about terrible things. But you can. Knowledge is power.

"We always did it up big in our old neighborhood," Ann says bringing me back to the present moment. She's very good at that. "But here, well, here... I noticed things are a bit more subdued."

"Subdued?" Clearly, she hasn't seen some of the women on our street with a few too many cocktails in them. Her last party hadn't really been that kind. Just wait. There is still time.

"Oh, you know..." she laments. But I'm not sure I do. "Quieter."

"You mean boring?"

Her eyes light up. "That's exactly what I mean."

"It looks fine," I assure her. "Subtle."

"Subtle." The word rests on her lips and she smiles. "That's a nice way to put it."

"So—coffee or tea...or gin?" she asks as she turns and opens the door. She holds it open for me.

"Coffee," I say thinking she is joking about the gin. It is hardly two in the afternoon. But when she fills her tumbler, I can see she isn't.

"How do you take it?"

"I'm sorry?"

"Your coffee."

"Oh." I twist the wedding ring I can't force myself to take off. *Around and around it goes.* She notices. "Black is fine."

"It's not just any coffee," she informs me. "It's from Jamaica." This is the part where she's going to tell me about her last trip there. I've heard the story secondhand. She surprises me instead. "And worth every penny it costs to import. I think you'll like it."

I'm sure, I tell her, and then I take account of all the other imported things I'm surrounded by. Her house looks different without everyone in it. She appears more relaxed, dressed in a sweater and jeans, same as me. Only hers are tailored and fit well, and of course, are at least a dozen sizes smaller.

"Crap," she says abruptly. She's leaning over a pan of Danishes she's just pulled from the oven. She fans them with her hand. "The butter I need for the glaze is in the garage." Ann looks up at me. "God—I miss my old house. Even the refrigerator was bigger."

"I can grab it," I offer, standing.

"Would you mind?"

"Not at all."

THE GARAGE IS WHERE THE GOOD STUFF IS, AND BY THAT I'M NOT just referring to the butter. Thinking of my predicament with the taillight on the way here, reminded me. If Ann hit that woman with her car, and I'm nearly certain she did, there will be evidence of it. Just in case this should all go south, I'll need proof. After all, a picture is worth a thousand words.

This, and I have to know.

Ann's car hasn't moved in days. It dawns on me that I've only seen her drive Paul's SUV, which she likes to do when he's away.

My pulse quickens as I retrieve my phone from my pocket. I use the flashlight to check Ann's front end for damage. There are minor scratches and a small dent, but as best I can see, no blood. No obvious bicycle paint. No broken headlights. I press the camera function to snap a photo, for later, in case I'm missing something. For now, I don't see anything that can't be explained away.

"Sadie?"

I jump. The sound of my pulse floods my ears. The hairs on the back of my neck make their presence known. All of my senses heighten.

It's Ann's voice, and she's close behind. I can't see her but I can smell her perfume. "I'm really sorry," she says. My chest tightens. "I sent you on a pointless mission. I found the butter inside."

"Oh."

Her hand comes to rest on my shoulder. "Is everything okay?"

"I dropped my wedding ring," I sigh.

"Your wedding ring?"

"I flung it off when I opened the refrigerator. I've been searching with the flashlight on my phone, and I still can't find it."

"Hmmm," she murmurs. "Why don't you just turn on the light?"

I shake my head as though the thought has just occurred to me.

She walks over to the wall, flips a switch, and suddenly a bright overhead light illuminates the space.

"There it is!" I exclaim, bending at the knee to retrieve it. "The cold makes it loose."

She steadies her gaze on mine. "Maybe you're losing weight."

"Fingers crossed," I laugh. It comes out disappointingly fake.

Ann offers a tight smile. "If they were crossed you wouldn't be in this predicament." She pivots fully in my direction. "Say, can I get a look at the photos you took the other night? I've been meaning to upload some to the neighborhood app."

She's referring to the photos from the dinner party. I'd only taken two. I wasn't aware she knew.

I hold my breath and hand her my phone. "Sure."

Ann smiles favorably as she takes the phone, and favor is exactly what I need right now. But I'm not thinking of that. I'm not thinking about how to explain this away or what I might say. I'm cataloging all of the weapons in this garage. I'm thinking of how I might defend myself.

"Got it," she says. "And...whoops. It looks like you snapped an extra one of my garage floor."

"Must have been while I was looking for my ring..."

She nods, and I do that thing every liar does where they offer more detail than the situation calls for. "I can't seem to manage even the simple things. I'm terrible at photography. I'm sure someone else took better photos."

"Maybe" she shrugs. "But I got what I needed—so you get the benefit of the doubt."

I manage a tight smile.

"Oh, and Sadie," Ann says. "There's something I've been thinking about..."

"Yeah?"

"There are cameras everywhere. We're never not being watched."

My breath catches in my throat. "Right."

"Which has me wondering...what kind of person do you think would be stupid enough to use their own car for a hit and run?"

"I wasn't aware they were planned," I answer brazenly, because sometimes Ann requires this.

She smiles. "You'd be surprised."

CHAPTER FIFTEEN

SADIE

Ann had to step out to take a call. Meanwhile, I've been pacing the kitchen, hoping my impetuousness hasn't ruined everything. "Sit," she demands when she returns. She places a cup of coffee in front of me. "I hope it's not gotten too cold. You'll let me know?"

I cup my hands around the mug, warming them. The coffee is perfect. Smells that way. Tastes that way. Not that I'd expected any less. I make sure to tell her as much. My nervousness makes me chatty, and I ask if everything went okay with the call.

She shrugs "You can never really be sure." She seems distracted.

"It must be difficult."

"Not really." I watch as she crosses the kitchen. She's very attractive when she's focused. Actually, she's always attractive. Just more so then. "Well—not in the way that most people think."

"What do you mean?"

"Oh, I don't know…" she stalls, and it's clear she's choosing her words carefully. "Sometimes my voice is the last they'll ever hear."

"That's sad," I say, sipping my coffee.

"Is it?"

"Well—"

"I was sorry to hear about what happened with your husband."

The abrupt manner in which she cuts straight to the bone causes me to choke on her perfect coffee. In her perfect home.

Black liquid spews across her white marble countertop. Maybe it's nerves on account of what just happened in the garage. Maybe it's something else entirely, but a lump has formed in my throat, making it impossible to swallow. I place the cup on the bar and make a start for the paper towel holder across the counter.

Ann waves me off. "Let me."

I settle in my seat as she cleans up after me. It makes me think of my mother.

"I can't imagine what it must be like."

"That's a good thing," I say, speaking around the lump, the way you learn to do with enough practice.

"But I can try."

"I wouldn't recommend it."

"I've lost things, too, you know. Not my husband. But things that were very important."

I nod, not only because I am uncomfortable. I hadn't expected her to be so blunt. No one else is. Not even in DUI class. At the same time, it bothers me. Ann speaks of Ethan as though he is dead. She makes it sound like he is never coming back. This reminds me. "The girl from yesterday…" I say. "Did she go through with it?"

Ann shakes her head. "Not yet. Probably tomorrow." I want to ask how she knows this. I want to ask a million questions, but before I get the chance, she goes on. "But that's not why I invited you over," she assures me. "I just wanted you to know that I'm sorry about your husband."

"Thank you." My gaze stays firmly fixed on the countertop. "These are nice," I say, tracing the granite, doing my best to change the subject.

"I want you to know that I'm here if you need to talk."

"I know," I tell her glancing up. "We are talking."

"Right." She looks away. She checks her phone. "I've been thinking about something a lot..." Her eyes meet mine and I'm terrified she's going to bring up the thing I know. The thing I am not ready for her to know. The thing that will ruin everything between us. "You need work, right?"

"Yes. Well, I mean...I've been subbing. But—"

"As I'm sure you're aware—not that I like to talk about it much, I find work terribly boring conversation—but my book has really taken off."

I lift the coffee cup and place it to my lips to keep me from saying something I'll regret. This is the part where I have to pretend not to know even though I do. Everyone around here knows. It's all anyone talks about. People trip over themselves just to be in her presence. She's the closest thing to famous this town's ever seen.

"I was thinking that maybe you'd want to help me in my business." She leans back against the counter and sizes me up. "I mean... when the subbing is slow. I can be flexible."

"What do you need?"

Her eyes narrow as though I've said the wrong thing. "So you know I'm a psychotherapist...but do you know what else I do?"

I know almost everything about you. "No."

"I help people, Sadie. Not just through my writing, or the hotline...but other ways too. A lot in my old life—before we came here."

While I consider what it is exactly that she's trying to tell me, she continues. "Kind of like..."

"Like yesterday at the coffee shop?"

"Sort of." Her eyes narrow. "I want to do more to give back—pro bono, of course."

I smile at her heart of gold.

"But I could pay you. Double, maybe even triple what they're paying you to sub."

All of a sudden, I feel like she can sense my desperation. The room starts to spin. Her lips are moving, I can hear her speaking, but the words come out muffled, jumbled and mixed together. I blink rapidly. I can feel myself doing it. Sometimes the anti-anxiety meds have this effect. Or maybe it's the anxiety. Either way, it causes time to slow. That—or she's put something in my coffee.

It's apparent that Ann is waiting for me to say something, probably something about how I'm like her, and I don't need the money. That I'm blessed to be able to do what I love just for the sake of doing it. That it comes from the goodness of my heart. But we both know that isn't true. Ann doesn't do it from the goodness of her heart either. It's just easier for her to pretend.

"There's one more thing," she says. "Neil was less than pleased with his English grade—to tell the truth, I really think his teacher has it out for him. Mrs. Terry. Do you know her?"

"Not very well."

"Huh," she says looking toward the door. "Well, it doesn't matter. Where there's a will, there's a way, right?"

"It's just one grade," I say, and the room goes on spinning.

"Not to Neil, it isn't. Not to Paul either. He's very hard on him. Too hard, if you ask me. But it is what it is. Anyway—we have high standards for our children, therefore they have high standards for themselves."

She says it like she doesn't quite believe what she's saying. "I can understand that."

"Can you?" Her expression is serious.

"Sure."

"Good," she tells me. "It'll make what I am about to ask you easier to swallow."

A quizzical look is offered meanwhile a rebuttal dances on my tongue.

"I need you to change his grade."

"I don't really have access to grades...I'm just a sub."

82

"But it's possible...say...next time you're in the office...to say...accidentally log in to the admin's computer. It wouldn't be too difficult. Would it? If, of course, you had the log-in information."

"Where would I get that?"

"Leave that to me. Let's say this is a test. Let's say I get you the information, and you change the grade, and if all goes well, you're hired."

I choke on my own spit. I'm amazed that Ann would ask me to do this. But then, maybe not really. "Sorry," I say when I finally get my bearings. I shake my head and push what's left of the coffee away. "It's really good. *Really* good," I lie. "But unfortunately, I think I've met my quota for today."

"It's pretty strong stuff." Ann flips on the faucet, fills a glass and hands it to me. "Anyhow—about the job—what I'm thinking —what I *need* is someone I can trust. Someone who will honor the very intimate details of my life. Someone to manage my schedule—"

"Like an assistant?" I'm surprised to hear my words slur.

"That's right. That way I can do what it is I do best—help people. Therapy is an amazing gift, Sadie. You should try it. I could even make it part of our deal, if you wanted. We could be... well, not *just* friends...but more. We could be partners."

The last time someone used the word therapy with me and spoke about how they wanted to do things like erase memories and replace them with other things, it hadn't turned out so well, so I say, "I'm not very good at therapy. And I'm not very good at organizing."

"Ah, now, Sadie. You shouldn't sell yourself short. You were the president of the yearbook club back in high school...you were at the top of your game at Norris and Tillman. That is, before you left to start a family."

I don't ask how she knows any of this. But she does, which makes any answer she might give too late.

"I've been accused of being an overachiever," I tell her. "In the past."

"By who?" Her brow furrows. "Underachievers?"

I laugh, and I realize she's the loveliest person I've ever met. "Something like that."

"All winners and losers in life are completely self-determined. But only the winners are willing to admit it. You can't let people justify their lack of success with criticism of your success. That's a surefire way to hell," she says. "And happiness isn't found there, trust me."

"I didn't start a family, though."

Ann rolls her eyes. "You have plenty of time."

"Hardly."

"Sadie. Sadie. Sadie." Her face twists like I'm missing a key clue to the universe. "Don't you know? You can have anything you want."

This causes me to scoff. I don't mean to. I'm afraid the people at that class are starting to rub off on me. "You don't know me."

"I know enough."

She's wrong about this, of course. Although, the confirmation that even people like her make mistakes is nice.

"Hang around me long enough," she says, "and you'll see."

My vision blurs, and the room is off kilter. Suddenly, I just want to go home and go to bed. I nod, but I don't know what I am supposed to see. I only know she is offering me something that seems of great value and that I want to accept it.

CHAPTER SIXTEEN

SADIE

I'm asleep. I'm awake. I'm sleeping while awake. I'm sleepwalking through life. I'd hardly made it through the front door. All I could think about was sleeping it off. I wanted to lie down in the middle of my floor, anything to make the spinning and the headache go away. I managed to make it to the couch, where closing my eyes brought sweet relief. I hadn't even bothered kicking off my shoes, apparently.

I slept for an eternity, for so long that when I wake, it feels a bit like I haven't slept at all. I feel delirious. I feel hung over. I feel stuck, half in this world, and halfway in another. My mouth is dry, my eyes are sticky, and my body aches in places I don't even recall being possible.

Part of me hadn't wanted to wake up. I had been dreaming of Ann. I dreamed we were digging. Digging a grave. Digging and digging. By we, what I really mean is, she was doing the watching. I was doing the heavy lifting.

While I was busy working up a sweat, Ann told me all about her life before she and her family moved to Penny Lane. Most of what she said was stuff I already knew. But her voice is lovely, and so long as she was talking, she wasn't killing me. So long as I was digging, I was still alive.

She told me her family were members of a church. By church I inferred that what she really meant was she was in a cult. Something I find so, so interesting. Not that she referred to New Hope as such. But that hasn't stopped the press—or the authorities—from doing it.

The details are hazy. It's a pity I can't recall the specifics of what she said, but dreams are rather like that, aren't they? The further I get from sleep, the hazier things become. There were, of course, some answers she wouldn't—or couldn't—give. Nor were they found in any of the reading I've done. So much reading.

I guess you can't really ever know everything about a person, can you?

Still, I suspect Ann did some shady things—things she's not proud of, things she wouldn't want anyone to know about. Not in her new life. Not with her growing fame. Which is why she didn't tell me about any of that. She doesn't trust me yet. I know because she accused me of spying on her. Before all of the digging started. Ann was livid. I promised—I pleaded with her—I wasn't. It was just...well, I figured since she knew so much about my history, that it was only fair if I learned a little more about hers. I explained that I want to know her. Really know her. I want to know everything. The bad, the good, and everything in between.

My response only half pleased her. She said I could have just as easily asked. She was right about this, obviously. I just figured why bother with awkward conversation—when you learn about a person via a simple internet search and a few phone calls? That's why spy novels set in present day aren't very interesting. How hard do you really have to work at it when everything is literally at your fingertips? Not very.

It wasn't hard to find out that Ann's husband is a surgeon, or that he works with charities like Medicine Without Borders, which is why he is frequently away. (She told me that much.) It wasn't hard to find out that she's a licensed therapist in the State of Texas. (She said that too.) It was all listed in her children's school records. Records I had easy access to, thanks to Ann's resourcefulness. She provided the admin password, after all.

What she didn't say, in my dream or in real life, was whether or not she is a murderer. Or is it murderess? Do we still live within an era where it's important to differentiate? Or is murder gender neutral too?

I don't know. What she did tell me was that since leaving New Hope, since the Feds had disbanded it, since the court had suspended her license, that she had set her sights on something better: becoming a guru of sorts. Ann has big dreams. Real dreams, not like mine. Dreams she's actually pursuing. She gives people advice on the internet for free, and she said it's amazing because you don't even have to have any sort of credentials to do it. But even if you do have them—and worse, they are stripped from you—likely for gross abuse and negligence— she says you don't have to worry. If you're good enough at deception, there's still hope in the land of the internet, where you can say what you want, and it's hard to be held accountable for anything.

But then, Ann doesn't know about social scoring the way I do.

I told her all about it as I dug my way to the center of the earth, in an empty field with only the light of the moon to guide us. She said it was the perfect team-building exercise—that if we were going to work together—if we were going to be friends—she had to know she could trust me. She said after the incident in the garage, her trust was buried way down deep, and if I wasn't careful, I might never see it again.

I threw out some accusations of my own, and it felt good. I told her I was aware that she's using me—that she needs a success story, and I know she thinks I can be it. *Look at me, look at what I've done. If I can help someone as wretched as Sadie transform, I can help you too.*

That's when she knelt down in the dirt beside me and cupped

my face with her hands. She stared directly into my eyes and told me I was wrong. She told me I was worthy of transformation. She said she was glad I brought my insecurity to her attention. She said this was a breakthrough for us. She said I was a dream. She said that just because two people see things differently doesn't mean they give up on each other. My feelings are normal. The truth sets you free, she said, but first it pisses you off. She said some things are hard to hear but those are usually the things worth knowing. And then, after she said all of that, she said the best and most important thing. She promised not to give up on me.

Afterward, right before I woke up, she asked if I hated her for making me do all of that digging. I assured her I didn't. And I don't. It wasn't a lie.

I understand the dream. I understand all of that digging served a purpose, and that it was a form of symbolism. She told me I was right—that there are many more qualified and capable women in the community she could have called upon for help. Women more like her. But she didn't ask any of them. She asked me.

CHAPTER SEVENTEEN

SADIE

I t's on nights like these that I really miss it, Sadie," Ann tells me wistfully. Paul is away, and she has a lot on her mind. I know this because she texted and asked me to join her for a glass of wine so we could finish discussing the details of our work together. Also, there is something she wanted me to see. Something "unbelievable."

"Austin?" I ask, thinking I'm glad she brought this up. It's a good time to gather some intelligence. It's a good time to see where her head is.

Ann has positioned her Adirondack chairs on her front porch so that they overlook the lane, which is really nice because it gives you a bird's eye view. It makes me feel otherworldly, one step beyond, sitting here beside her. "That—and just—well...home."

"I hadn't really thought about it. I guess for me...this is home."

"Really? Doesn't it ever just all feel the same to you?"

I take a moment to consider what she is asking. "Well, the houses are constructed similarly."

"Not the houses," she says. "The people. Life. Every day. It's all the same."

"Hmmm. I haven't given it much thought..."

"Well, now's the time, Sadie..."

I watch as she nurses her glass of red. Something is clearly bothering her, but like most women, Ann isn't the type to just spit it out.

She hasn't yet noticed I'm not drinking, and I hope she won't. I've already pegged the potted plant meant for the contents of my glass just as soon as I can divert her attention. After last night, drinking anything in her presence doesn't seem like the smartest thing to do. "Look at my lights..." she points. "This is a disaster."

I do look. A few bulbs are blown—maybe a quarter of them—actually, an entire strand or two, but it's not what I'd call a *disaster*.

She runs her hands over the length of her face, pausing to massage her temples. "Wait until Paul comes home."

It's the first time I've seen her look anything close to tired. "This is unacceptable," she tells me. "He works so hard, Sadie. So hard. I only wish you knew what he has to deal with. The least I can do is make things bright and cheery for him when he comes home. The least."

"I don't think—"

Her eyes focus in on me. Her stare is icy and cold. Heartless. "That's right, Sadie. You don't think."

"I—"

"I paid the guy to purchase and install my holiday lighting. And you know what's missing? THE LIGHTING, SADIE. The lighting is missing."

"I'm sure if you called him..."

Her cheeks are flushed, and I don't think it's the wine. She cocks her head first, and then her brow follows as though on command. "You think I haven't thought of that?"

"Well, I—"

"What do you take me for?"

"It's just—"

She cuts me off, lowering her voice to a near whisper. "I wanted our first Christmas here to be perfect. That bastard—"

I press my lips together tightly in an attempt to suppress a smile. I can't help myself. I'm almost amused by her anger at something so...so...trivial. It isn't like her. Everywhere I go I can't get away from hearing about how great she is. How kind and lovely. How she's changing the world by motivating the masses. And yet, here and now, live and in color, she's nothing at all like she portrays herself to be in public. Her emotions have hairpin turns. "Maybe—"

"There is no maybe. He gypped me. Claims he can't fit me in his schedule for another two weeks. Paul will be home well before then, and the holidays will be half over." She lets out a long and heavy sigh. "And then there's the Christmas party to think about..."

"It'll all work out."

She looks at me like I'm crazy. The way my husband used to. "What's the point?"

This time I smile, because she is not the person everyone thinks she is—and not just because she may or may not be a murderer either. This is not sunny Ann; this is not the cheerleader for all. This is someone who cares deeply what other people think and is desperately trying to hide it.

I do my best to redirect the conversation. Something that should feel familiar to Ann—a trick right out of her own book. "I don't see how you find the time."

"Are you kidding? I have nothing but time."

"What about your work?"

"This is work, Sadie. That's why you're here."

Her words sting. I'm still learning the boundaries of our relationship. The borders aren't quite mapped out. *Are we friends? Or am I just her employee?*

"Are you writing?"

"Only every second of every day. But it's not enough, Sadie. It's never enough."

I don't know what she means. Although, I want to. I want to

know how I dig my claws further into this situation the way Ann would, if she were me, so I ask what's stopping her.

"Oh, you know... life..." She tells me as she fingers the stem of her glass. "Paul is away so much, and the kids need at least one of us around...especially at this age."

"Right."

"It's nothing new. You know, just the old 'how to make it all work without fucking up the kids' conundrum."

I *don't* know, actually. I probably never will. Still, I do my best to pretend by agreeing profoundly. "I absolutely get it," I say. "It's such an impressionable time in their lives. They do need you around. I see it all the time when I sub. You can always pick out the ones who are lacking in the parenting department."

Once again, she looks at me as though I've lost my mind. She was expecting me to disagree. She was expecting me to try and fix it. I know better. There will be plenty of time later on for offers of help with the ins and outs. For now, the seed has been planted. With any luck, it will grow and grow and grow. I just have to water it and care for it until it's time for harvest.

"It seems pointless sometimes, doesn't it?"

"Pointless? No, I don't think so."

Ann visibly softens. "I'm glad I have you in my life, Sadie. It's nice to have someone who gets it," she says and sometimes the harvest comes sooner than you think.

"If you want...I could bring over a ladder and check the wiring on the lights. I used to help my dad a lot as a kid."

"Really?"

"He was an electrician," I tell her and it's only a partial lie. The best kind usually are. Little bit of fact. Little bit of fiction. My dad wasn't an electrician. To hear my mother tell it, he hardly worked at all. But he did come over and hook us in to the neighbor's grid once, when our electricity was cut. It was the least he could do, said my mother. He saved the day, and he asked me to be his apprentice. So the next time, he said, I would be able to do it on my own. I thought he was joking. I didn't know him well enough to know, he wasn't.

Ann's eyes narrow. "I couldn't ask you to do that."

"It's no trouble," I tell her. "Probably just a loose bulb somewhere."

She gazes out at the lane. I can see that she's considering something deeply. I don't think it's the lights. "I don't know...it seems like a lot to ask..."

"No promises," I say in the spirit of under promising and over delivering. Just like she says to do in her book. "But I'll try."

Finally, her eyes meet mine. "Thanks, Sadie. You're a gem."

"It's nothing, really. And, hey, if I can't figure it out, I'll just have to find your lighting guy and force him to fix it."

Her whole demeanor shifts then. She stares at me for a long while without saying anything. Eventually, she motions between the two of us. "Don't you just love this?"

"Yes," I say, and I find that I actually kind of mean it.

She finishes off her glass. "Whether everything around here feels the same or not—it's really good to have a friend. To have someone who understands you—well, I don't know what's better than that."

"You have a lot of friends." I don't mean to say this out loud. It's just that I have that annoying warm and fuzzy feeling in the pit of my stomach, and I'm not being careful.

I expect her to either affirm or contradict what I've said the way most people would. But Ann is smarter than that. She goes at it from another angle. "I always find that this time of year holds so much promise."

"It really does."

"This time of evening is my favorite."

"Mine too," I lie. It's surprising how easy it is becoming to tell her what she wants to hear. The truth is, nighttime is the absolute worst. Every absence is felt more keenly after the sun goes down. The rest of my evening is mapped out like it was written in the stars long ago. First, I'll Google Weight Watchers, and then, if I'm really feeling desperate, I'll search for more drastic measures. Diets that suggest it's possible to lose ten pounds in a week. Later, after I've had my fill of before and after photos, I'll swear that tomorrow I won't eat the chips, or the cookies, or buy the expensive coffee with all of the poison and the calories. I make myself believe that tomorrow, I'll look for a better job. Tomorrow I'll become a new person.

But like Ann pointed out before the wine made her a liar, tomorrow always turns out just the same.

CHAPTER EIGHTEEN

HER

R-E-S-P-E-C-T. *Find out what it means to me*. Aretha's voice crackles over the cheap radio he takes on his jobs. He sings along, his face is fixed in concentration as he readies his tools. I have to admit, his enthusiasm is inspiring. I can't help but hum along quietly too. Funny, he knows the song. But missed the meaning.

Her dissatisfaction over the holiday decor was evident. No one should be upset at Christmas—and I can't blame her for wanting things to be perfect. She has a lot riding on it.

Just a little bit.

He mouths the words into his hammer before shoving it into his tool belt, which he fastens around his waist. Then he inspects his work area. When he's satisfied, he climbs the ladder confidently, deftly. He's a man on a mission—squeezing as many jobs as he can into a short window of time. Chasing the almighty dollar, he cuts corners where he can.

Safety should not be one of those corners. A split-second decision—like, say…whether to put on a harness or not—can mean the difference between life and death.

Shortcuts are everywhere these days. Mediocrity runs

rampant. It's just such a shame he takes this particular short cut on a day like today.

Because life is actually very precise. The angle at which a ladder stays upright and the angle at which it tips is pretty exact. It's possible to sustain a fall from that height and survive. But then, so is honoring your word.

CHAPTER NINETEEN

SADIE

I didn't see Ann knock the Christmas light guy off his ladder with my own four eyes (I lost my contacts again, don't ask) but what else could explain him breaking *both* his legs *and* his back just one day after our conversation? That doesn't even take into account the coma and the brain bleed.

Such a shame, Ann said when she called to tell me the news. Now he'll never get back here, and I really do need you, Sadie. That's what she said. *He'll never get back here.* Thirteen thousand people fall each year in the United States, alone, hanging holiday lights.

Ann knows this, so I know this.

Can you believe that, she demanded to know over the phone.

I can believe it. I can especially believe it from the vantage point of her roof while trying to find what is causing the outage of half of her lights. Turns out, one of the connectors had become loose. Wind, likely.

When I call down to her to let her know that I've found the issue, she doesn't seem surprised. She says it was probably the high wind that caused the lighting guy to fall. She hollers up that she's just received a text. He died on the operating table.

I say the alphabet in my head. Over and over. It helps to distract myself. To remind me of what's at stake. Heights are not my favorite thing.

It's probably better that way, Ann calls up in response to my silence. She tells me it's better than the alternative. I don't ask what she means. I'm too afraid I might find out something I'm not yet ready to know.

CHAPTER TWENTY

SADIE

The holiday lighting guy's death makes the local news but not for the reasons you might think. The headline reads: The Danger of Christmas.

Never mind that somewhere out there, there's a widow. Somewhere a family is without. A man is dead, and the local media wants you to know there's a better way. Their spin: Don't be the fall guy.

When I express my outrage to Ann, she tells me I'm being ridiculous. The story was probably sponsored by a competitor, she says. Brilliant marketing, she says. That's exactly how she'd play it, she says.

The dangers of Christmas. Can't be too careful. Better to leave the decorating to a professional. If they screw up, it's on them.

I know a thing or two about that. A few days later, when Ann calls to invite me to be her plus one to an event, I screw up by not agreeing right away. I can tell by her response: Never mind. She'll just ask Darcy. When I remind her that she doesn't even like Darcy, she hangs up on me, forcing me to call her right back and ask what I should wear.

I can hear the smugness in the pace of her breath. "Dress nice," she tells me. "Business casual."

"I don't—"

"You need this, Sadie. You don't know it. But you do. It'll be good for you. For us. Stick with me, and you'll see. I make things happen."

I don't ask what kind of things. Maybe I should have.

Instead, I'm too busy thinking about the fact that she asked me to be her plus one *first* and what this means. I am reminded of that story in her book about living with purpose—where she talks about how if you add the wrong things in the wrong order, everything gets messed up. I'm beginning to realize that's what happened with Ethan and me.

Ann tells the story like this:

A philosophy professor once stood before his class with a large empty mayonnaise jar. He filled the jar to the top with large rocks and asked his students if the jar was full.

The students said that yes, the jar was indeed full.

He then added small pebbles to the jar, and gave the jar a bit of a shake so the pebbles could disperse themselves among the larger rocks. Then he asked again, "Is the jar full now?"

The students agreed that the jar was still full.

The professor then poured sand into the jar to fill up any remaining empty space. The students agreed that the jar was now completely full.

The professor went on to explain that the jar represents everything that is in one's life. The rocks are equivalent to the most important stuff in life, such as spending time with your family and maintaining proper health. This means that if the pebbles and the sand were lost, the jar would still be full, and your life would still have meaning.

The pebbles represent the things in your life that matter, but that you could live without. The pebbles are certainly things that give your life meaning (such as your job, house, hobbies, and friendships), but they are not critical for you to have a meaningful life. I don't agree about the job part—something tells me Ann Banks has never known a life of unemployment. But I digress. Her point is, these things often come and go, and are not permanent or essential to your overall well-being. So, she's partially correct. I'll give her that.

Finally, the sand represents the remaining filler things in your life. This could be small things such as social media or fake friends or other people's opinions. These things don't mean much to your life as a whole, and focusing on them is likely only done to waste time.

The metaphor here is that if you start with putting sand into the jar, you will not have room for rocks or pebbles. This holds true with the things you let into your life. If you spend all of your time on the small and insignificant things, you will run out of room for the things that are actually important.

It makes sense now why she got so angry before. Ann invited me because I'm important to her. She's asking me to be her rock.

Now, she's clearing her throat, and she's asking me if I'm even listening. I am.

"You need to get out of the house..." she states. "Meet people."

"It's not as easy for some of us," I reply, thinking of the sand, considering what she says about fillers. "I'm not good with people."

"Now, Sadie..." Her tone is laced with warning. "Don't confuse the truth with an excuse."

"I'm not."

"Good, so you'll come, then?"

"Yes," I answer. I can hear the smile in her voice.

And that is that.

CHAPTER TWENTY-ONE

SADIE

Ann tricks me. We aren't going to some literary luncheon, as I'd assumed. Nope. She takes me to a funeral. Her lighting guy's to be exact. When I protest, Ann brushes it off. She says the experience will be good for us. She says we can do hard things together. It's not in her book, that platitude. I checked. She says strong winds grow strong roots. She tells me she intends to tell the man's widow this in person. I think she's joking, but with her you never know.

Her good mood and her good looks wear on me. She looks amazing, in a made-up, sensational kind of way—a way that knows it will be looked at and appreciated. It's the best I've seen her, actually. Her hair is down and it falls in waves around her pale and delicate face, past her shoulders, very nearly touching the small of her back. By the time most women reach Ann's age, they've long since chopped their hair off. Usually into a neat little bob, or as they say, into something more manageable. But not her.

I ask her about it, and she tells me she'd rather die first—and that likely the cause would be boredom. Who wants something manageable, she asks. Where's the fun in that?

Ann appreciates transcendence, she says, which is why she's

obsessed with funerals. She crashes them like weddings. Or at least, she tells me, she used to—when she had more time, by which she means *before she was famous*.

Already, I am not a fan. But then, no one I ever knew could afford to be buried properly, so Ann tells me it's not like I can be sure.

"Lighting guy," as she refers to him, has an open casket, which makes me pretty sure, pretty quick. His real name is Darryl, and his funeral is quiet and depressing. Family members and friends sit shoulder to shoulder, tight-lipped and tense, in rows divided by a long aisle. It's like a wedding, only less joyous, a house divided with his and her families on either side.

Death brings out the worst in people.

Ann knows this, so I know this.

It's amazing, what they can do with makeup, Ann says.

Embalming is a very clinical process, Ann says.

It takes less time than you might think—she explains. The actual embalming only takes between forty-five minutes and an hour. But dressing the body and the application of makeup...well, depending on the circumstance, that can take a lot longer. They take as much care as possible, Ann says. It's important to make sure the body is respected. It's important to ensure that decomposition is slowed down as much as possible, and that the body is returned to its most lifelike and natural state. A relaxed, natural-looking body is much less traumatic for loved ones, especially where the deceased died in a traumatic way.

Darryl's death was very traumatic.

As we near the casket—it's the respectful thing to do, Ann assures me—she points to his chest. Touch it, she says. I don't. It doesn't stop her.

"You see?" she whispers. "They use paper to puff up his chest."

"Really?"

"Yeah—for one, his ribs were crushed when he fell. But also, they removed most of his organs."

It doesn't feel like an appropriate time to inquire about how she knows all of this. She just does, and apparently, she wants to make sure I know too. This is why she goes on. "Once your body is filled with embalming fluid, it's nearly impossible to make any adjustments. So, they have to set your facial features first."

Someone walks up to the casket and stands shoulder to shoulder with us. Ann stops talking. Her expression turns somber.

"Rest in peace," the woman says to Darryl. She leans down and kisses his forehead. She moves on.

"They use photos to make sure they get as close to a natural looks as possible," Ann says, peering into the casket. "Did you ever meet Darryl?"

I shake my head. She knows this.

"That's too bad. I assure you they did a good job."

Ann touches my arm, and I think finally she's ready to move along. "His eyes are kept closed by small pieces of cotton. Can you imagine?"

I can't. I hate cotton.

"You see there…" she motions. "His jaw is wired shut. They even stitch your lips together. Although, they use glue more and more these days. Less work, that way."

Later after we're seated, Ann tells me about the moisturizer that is applied to prevent drying, to ensure a lifelike, relaxed appearance. "I bet they don't use the cheap stuff, either," she sighs. "What a waste," she says. "All of this for the living."

Eventually, the elevator music stops and people begin taking their seats. As the room fills up, Ann reaches over and intertwines her fingers with mine. She squeezes my hand. "I'm so glad you came, Sadie. You have no idea how much I need you."

"No problem," I manage to say, willing her with the power of my mind to move her hand away. Her touch is electrifying and being needed is terrifying. I remember what happened the last time I felt this way, and it didn't end well. Only Ann doesn't move her hand. In fact, unless I'm imagining things, she shifts in her seat so that she is closer, so that her thigh rests against mine.

My chest tightens like all of the little air pockets closing up, and it's all I can do to hang on for the ride. I don't want to breathe. I don't want to move. I know this feeling. This feeling makes me do very stupid things. Like open my mouth when I really, really shouldn't. "She doesn't seem that sad does she?" I whisper to Ann forcing the air from my lungs. "Darryl's wife."

"She had a hefty life insurance policy. She'll be fine."

I ask her how she knows this.

"People talk, Sadie," she answers and then she looks over at me. She leans closer until I can practically feel her lips move against my ear. "Sometimes," she explains. "The only way out of a bad marriage is till death actually does *do* you part."

I shift in my seat. "He was only forty something…"

"You can't be sad about everyone who dies. None of us are meant to live forever."

Her thumb strokes mine. I scan the room and pray this is over soon.

"Divorce," she tells me, "is so expensive. And no one wins, in the end."

I think of Ethan. "I don't like funerals."

"Oh Sadie," she chides. "For heaven's sake. Don't be such a baby."

"I'm not being anything."

"You need to get comfortable with death."

"Nobody is comfortable with death," I argue.

"I am. Don't you see? This is proof that we all get what's coming to us, and it's so fucking beautiful, don't you think?"

My mouth hangs open. I don't know what to think.

Ann pulls her hand from mine. "Jesus. You're as white as a ghost. Don't take everything so seriously." Her voice is flustered. "I'm just kidding."

"Ethan's parents are the beneficiaries of his life insurance policy. If he passed, I'd get nothing."

"Is that what's bothering you?" she asks, and she sort of half-laughs, almost mockingly.

"No, not really."

"Good." Her lips press to one another. I can't take my eyes off of them and I hate myself for it. "That just means they'd all have to die together."

She looks like she's joking. But I can't be sure she is.

"You didn't know him, did you?" a booming voice asks. Ann is up front, near the casket, speaking to the family, and I am standing at the door pretending to study all the pamphlets. *A fish out of water.* I'm ready to get out of here. My plus one, however, seems to feed off the attention. They hang around her like moths, so much so that I was desperate to break away. Everyone tells her how wonderful it was that she took time out of her busy schedule to pay her respects. They say it shows her true character. She beams. She's in her element. I feel like a hunted animal, banished to the outskirts.

"I'll take that as a no," the voice says, and it's then that I realize he is speaking to me. When I turn, a man in a suit and tie, both of which are about two sizes too big, is peering down at me. "You're a faker."

"And you? What are you? The doorman?"

"Ah. Funny," he remarks, and when he smiles, the deep lines around his eyes crinkle. "No, just a friend." He shoves his hands in his pockets and balances on his heel and still he towers over me. His green eyes search mine, for what I'm not sure. For a soul, or perhaps just a response. I make a point to focus on the gold flecks in his eyes just so I don't get lost. He extends his hand, and for a second, or maybe an eternity, it's suspended in the air between us, just hanging. "I'm Chet."

"I'm the friend of a friend."

He glances toward the front of the funeral home. "Are you coming by the house?"

"Me." A pause. Then, I shake my head and tell him decisively, "no."

"That's too bad."

"I don't like funerals," I say, because—nerves.

"There's food."

"That I do like."

He laughs. It's a deep and genuine laugh, and I get the sense that most things about him are that way, and that he's the kind of guy you shouldn't walk away from. You should run.

Eventually, Ann joins us. "Chet," I say. "This is Ann."

"It's a pleasure," he says. They shake hands. I don't know if he knows who Ann Banks is. If he does, he doesn't say, and his expression gives nothing away.

"So, you're really not coming by the house?"

I shake my head. He looks from me to Ann and back. She doesn't notice. She's scrolling her phone. Ann doesn't care for Chet, and she isn't very good at hiding it. When I introduced them, she shook his hand with the kind of look in her eye that said she planned to tell me all about it later.

Meanwhile, he seems oblivious. Like he couldn't care less about beating a dead horse. He doesn't know her, clearly. "How will I see you again?"

"I'm married," I say. "And this is a small town."

"Yeah, well," he says. "Exactly—and I'm down a friend."

CHAPTER TWENTY-TWO

SADIE

The holidays draw nearer, and Ann gains in popularity. Not just among her social following, but also among women in our neighborhood. She's the new kid on the block and everyone is interested in something new. Myself included.

Judging by the comings and goings at her house, it's only a matter of time before she doesn't need me anymore. I know I can't let that happen. It didn't turn out well for the guy at the grocery store—or the caterer—or the guy who hung her Christmas lights.

Speaking of, her Christmas party is the first time I see her in a new light. While most of the homes on Penny Lane have undergone substantial renovations, the Bankses' was torn down completely and rebuilt from the ground up. Ann wanted that. If she had to downsize, she said—if she had to move to the middle of nowhere—she might as well design the place the way she wanted.

What she wanted, she said, was something that blended fine on Penny Lane but was just unique enough that it stuck out.

Looking at it now, it's obvious she was successful in her aspirations. She lives in a breathtaking Mediterranean-style home, one of the largest on our street. The kind of place everyone gravitates toward. Myself included.

"Thank God you're here," Ann tells me as she swings open the door. Donning a black sweater dress, which only makes her red hair stand out more, and thigh high boots, she looks amazing. She looks like fire. She looks exactly like what she is—something that will burn you if you get too close but is just warm enough that you can't help yourself.

Ann has minimal curves, but she doesn't let that stop her. She accentuates her straight lines and her hard edges with a matching personality. I recall Ethan mentioning once, after she and Paul had stopped by the lane to check on the renovations, that she has the look of a super model that has aged well. Lean and well preserved. She told us at her dinner party that where she came from, that was important. No one asked what she meant. We all made our own assumptions. Or at least I did.

"You look great," I say, which is a truth we both know. I assume her dress is cashmere. It looks precisely like that brand of perfect. She seems to read my mind because she says, "Go ahead and touch it," and I learn I'm right. As my fingertips brush against the fabric, my eyes close involuntarily. Instantly, I am transported to another time and another place.

"Isn't it just the softest thing you've ever felt?"

"Yes," I lie. But when I open my eyes Ann has her gaze fixed on mine with such intensity that I add, "Ethan, he has soft, curly hair. It feels a bit like that."

"Hmmm. I have an idea for you." She takes me by the elbow and hurls me through the door. It's a portal into her world where all is perfect and right and husbands who leave always come back.

I stumble though the entryway, mostly because I'm not used to wearing heels. She takes notice, which gives me the chance to get my bearings. Her eyes narrow as she gives me the once-over. "Nice dress."

I don't think she really means it about the dress, which is

disappointing because the tag is jabbing me between the shoulder blades, an ever-present reminder that it has to go back where it came from. "You think so?"

"I mean, it's not my taste, but I will say this: if your husband sees you looking like that, he'll regret his decision and come running back in a heartbeat."

"Maybe."

"Here," she says, pulling out her phone. She leans in close and snaps a selfie. Her perfume smells nice. It's imported from France, she tells me, by which I know she means it's out of my budget. "Let's tilt the odds in our favor."

Her eyes carefully scan the photo on her screen. She isn't pleased. With one hand she drops the phone to her side and with the other she pushes my back against the wall. I start to resist but then she presses a finger against my lips and I stop. I let go long enough to search her face, and she lets her finger drop too. Slowly. Too slowly. I have no idea what she's up to, or what's gotten into her, but I can think of worse ways to die.

While I'm wondering what I said, what I've done, what I'm about to do, she busies herself tangling her fist in my hair. Next thing I know, she is parting my mouth open with her tongue, and she is lingering there. I don't know how long a moment can last. Time is irrelevant. Meaningless. Until it isn't. Because quickly— too quickly—she pulls away, and then it's over. A void remains where her lips have been. No one has kissed me like that. Not ever.

Her back rests against the wall beside me; she's breathless. Finally, she lets out a long satisfied sigh, leans in close, tilts her head, and snaps another photo. She holds it up for me to see. "Perfect."

"Please don't post that."

Ann glances at the screen and then over at me and back. "Why not? It's a great photo. You see? You have to feel love before you can have love. Desire is the same. The look on your face...Sadie. That's what men want."

I want to ask if that's what she wants. I say the next most stupid thing instead. "Ethan isn't on social media."

"Oh, Sadie," she chides. "This isn't about social media. This is about revenge."

I shrug. Maybe she's right. Maybe Ethan will see it. Maybe he'll get really lonely and Google me, and there it will be. Me in my new life. Me with my new friends. Not the wife he remembers. Better.

And if not, well, there's always the off chance he'll hear the news secondhand. We still have some mutual friends from college, if that's what you call the people you're connected with on social media but never actually speak to.

"Don't worry," Ann says. "If that doesn't do it, there's always the neighborhood app."

I smile because she makes a good point. Ethan used to check that religiously when we moved here.

"He'll see it," she assures me.

I bite my lip, and then I force a smile. Ethan never cared much for social media but maybe that changed. A lot of things had changed.

CHAPTER TWENTY-THREE

SADIE

My key isn't even halfway in the lock when I realize something is very, very wrong. My heart hitches in my throat. There's movement inside. It suddenly dawns on me that the porch is dark, and I know for sure I left the light on.

Slowly, I pull the key from the lock. Every fiber of my being is telling me to turn and run. But then, I hear music coming from inside, and I realize I'm probably overreacting. It's probably just Ethan, but I'm in no mood for his games. We're playing on my terms now.

As I retreat, I consider going back to the party, and what I'll say when I do. *I'm afraid to go home. Someone's in my house. It could be my husband.*

I'm halfway up the walk when the door suddenly flings open. Just inside, there's the outline of a man. I can see that he's holding something in his hand, although I can't make out what that thing is. Partially because I'm blinded by the light behind him but, also, because I've taken off in full sprint.

I had no idea I could run so fast. Unfortunately, it isn't fast enough. I don't even make it to the end of the driveway before I feel his fingertips grasping at my shoulder. Winded, and practically caught, I do the thing that makes least amount of sense, I turn and take a swing at him.

He ducks.

I take another swing but he evades it just the same. "Sadie!"

I can't place the voice.

"Sadie, stop!"

Finally, under the glow of the street lamp, I get a look at his face. "You!"

"Sadie," he says through bated breath.

"Chet?"

"Jesus," he pants. "Why'd you run?"

I fold, bracing my palms on my knees. "Why are you chasing me?"

"I heard you fumbling with the lock. I bolted the deadbolt just so I wouldn't scare you—in case you weren't expecting me. Although, I was told you would be."

I stand and meet him face to face. "What are you doing in my house?"

His brow furrows. "Your husband hired me to paint."

"He what?"

"Well, actually he hired Darryl. But...you know how that turned out."

I mull over what he's said. Maybe Ethan told me he'd hired someone and maybe he hadn't. I'm pretty sure he hadn't. "Come see," he says. "I'm sorry I scared you."

My living room is chaos. Paint fumes fill my house, which Chet seems to think he can cover up by playing classical music. All of my furniture has been covered and moved to one side of the living room. Nothing is as I left it or as it's supposed to be.

"You look nice," Chet tells me.

I look at him as though he's lost his mind and I breathe in hard in an attempt to keep the tears at bay. I feel them stinging the back of my throat, building. Until suddenly they're out and I'm sobbing and I can't stop. I press the heels of my hands against my eye sockets but it makes little difference. Giant chest-heaving sobs pull me under. "I don't understand," I manage to choke out. "It wasn't supposed to go this way."

Chet sighs, obviously at a loss for words. He doesn't get it. His presence is proof. My life is over. I'm going to be homeless soon. The thought of standing on a street corner does something inside. It's like a dam breaks and the floodgates have opened and God help anyone downstream.

Finally, I sink to the floor. Not dramatically or anything. Just in a way that points out there is nowhere else to sit. I don't notice when he comes to my aid. All I know is I feel him kneel beside me. "Are you okay?"

He pats my back like one might a child, rubbing in small circles the way my mother used to do. It only makes me cry harder. "Can I get you something?"

I shake my head. "This was not how it's supposed to go."

"It's a small town," he whispers. "It was inevitable."

I look up at him, confusion playing across my face. "What was?"

"Me seeing you again."

I don't offer a response. He forces a handkerchief into my hand. It smells like aftershave and sweat and something else...the earth, maybe. Whatever it is, it reminds me of the dirt I used to play in with my mother, while she worked in her clients' flowerbeds. She did the planting. I did the digging.

Chet stands and gives me space. I cry harder, thinking of those days. I can't recall how long it has been since I let myself go there. But I go there now, picturing my mother, tending someone else's flowers, someone else's children, someone else's husband. I used to wonder if she wanted those things to be hers.

Now, I know she did.

Suddenly, I am aware of Chet's movement, of his presence, of his breath. For several moments, he just stands there with his hands on his hips as though he is contemplating what to do about the mess he's found himself in. At some point I feel him move away. Eventually, he reaches for my hand and I see that he has uncovered the sofa. He motions for me to take a seat. "I can come back later," he tells me. "If you prefer."

"It's fine," I manage. "So Ethan hired you to paint." It's not really a question, more like a realization. Chet misses that.

"Not just paint." He lists off the projects he is contracted to complete.

I nod and with it comes a long and heavy sigh. So my husband is going to sell the house. Somehow I knew this was coming.

But the finality of it lands hard. Something breaks loose inside of me, and the tears find their way back to the surface.

CHAPTER TWENTY-FOUR

SADIE

Chet comes back the next day. And the next after that. He paints the living room. He finishes. He starts on the bedrooms. He finishes those too. He works fast. Too fast.

He does his best to stay out of my way. He tries to be polite. Still, his mere presence makes me furious. It's amazing how fast it is to go from a slight dislike to strong hatred. This doesn't go unnoticed by him. We have entire conversations with our eyes. I guess there's some part of you who knows, *just knows,* when someone is going to upend your life. When someone *is* upending your life.

It doesn't help that my disdain seems to amuse him more than anything, which, of course, only infuriates me more. He laughs when I ask him to park his work truck around the corner. He goes so far as to throw his head back in the process. "Sweetheart," he says. "If you're worried about what the neighbors think at this stage in your life, you've got bigger problems than you think."

I tell him to fuck off.

"The kitchen is next," he replies, moving into my space, leaning too close, whispering into my ear. "A complete remodel, I hear."

"That makes one of us," I say, moving away. I sort the mail

while he stands at the sink, washing his brushes. I catch my mind wandering. I catch myself watching his hands. I hate his hands. I hate his broad shoulders and his crooked smile and his unending enthusiasm about the way my life is unfolding. His presence has worn grooves in my understanding. Ethan is easing me into the idea of losing him, just like my mother did.

Chet senses me watching him. He glances up and then over at me. It's nothing out of the ordinary. He's used to me watching him. He seems to read my expression and he smiles wryly. "Come on. Tell me you at least like the color."

"Does it matter?"

"It does to me." The sincerity in his voice sounds like poison. And yet, it makes me take a second look. I'm not expecting him to appear as genuine as he does. It forces me to reassess what I'm dealing with. It forces me to *really* look at him—maybe for the first time.

I gather he's in his late forties, not that I've ever been good at guessing that sort of thing. He's seen a day or two in the sun, for sure, which makes it hard to tell. At any rate, he's fit, very fit, and although his face is moderately symmetrical, it's not enough to classify him as handsome. Nevertheless, he has that blue-collar, hardworking look going for him. That, combined with his height, broad shoulders, and a strong jaw—well, I'd be willing to bet he does all right.

"Did you always want to be a carpenter?"

"Always," he says. "But my parents had other plans. They wanted me to go into banking. Like my old man. So I did for a while."

"Didn't take?" I ask.

He shakes his head. "Most things that aren't meant to be don't."

∾

THAT EVENING CHET ASKS IF IT'S OKAY IF HE STAYS LATE TO WORK on the grout. The cabinets have been delayed coming in and he tells me it's going to cost him time. For him, time is money. I thank God for small favors.

But I say yes, because it beats spending the evening alone. I cook Chicken Marsala. Partly because it's Ethan's favorite and I hope it gets back to him somehow. Also, I'm hungry, and I want to slow Chet's progress by being in his way the same as he's in mine.

It works, apparently. A little Italian food paired with two glasses of wine, a fire, and well…the next thing I know, Chet is stripping me out of my good underwear, and I am letting him.

This isn't a good idea, I'm thinking, as his hand slides up my shirt. I *know* it isn't a good idea when he shoves my panties aside and gets to know the other, more enjoyable parts of me. But by the time he lays me back onto the couch and the plastic that covers it sticks to my back as he explores my good side with his tongue, I give absolutely zero fucks. I convince myself there's no such thing as a bad idea, and anyway, I can't help myself. Not even if I wanted to. How else am I supposed to get rid of him?

My moves are calculated. Same as him, it seems. There's no surer way to get fired than fucking the wife of the man who hired you to fix his house, no matter how bad their relationship might be. Plus, the longer I delay renovations, the longer I have a home. And the longer I have a home, the longer I have a shot at keeping my marriage.

So we fuck. We laugh. We keep it light. We tiptoe around anything of substance. Besides food. I'm considerate enough to feed him before he fucks me. Men seem to like that. Eventually, when we both run out of fucks to give, Chet leaves. I intentionally don't ask him to stay the night. That would be far too convenient.

And yet, it doesn't stop me from meeting him at the door the following morning wearing a smile and not much else. "I want you to fuck me like you did last night," I say to him. It doesn't even sound like me, even as the words topple out of my mouth. It sounds like something Ann would say, which only widens my smile and apparently, his too.

He shrugs and drops his sack lunch. "You're the boss."

I was afraid he might tell me no. I was afraid he might tell me that I had been right the night before, that *this* wasn't a good idea. But he doesn't. He simply lays his tools down and gets down to business.

Chet's a good lover, as I knew he would be. He takes his time, working me meticulously and thoroughly, the same way he works on my house. He seems genuinely interested in what turns me on, which isn't even a requirement for what we're doing. He's eager and enthusiastic—a deadly combination when you know something is short lived.

He makes me crave him in a way he doesn't yet realize is dangerous. Beginnings are usually like that.

But this is different.

This isn't a beginning. Not really.

I know because afterward, he says, "I hope this doesn't change things between us."

"Why would it?" I ask.

He answers with a shrug. But it turns out, neither one of us are very good liars. It changes everything.

CHAPTER TWENTY-FIVE

SADIE

"You're a godsend, Sadie. A true godsend. Lord knows you can't get much out of teenagers these days." Ann has asked me to help her set up for her New Year's Eve party. How she is managing to host not *one*, but *two* big parties in the span of a week is beyond everyone. It's all anyone on Penny Lane and everyone on our neighborhood app can talk about. Ann, and her parties. Ann, and how amazing she is.

Little do they know, she has a secret weapon to do most of the work: me. I don't mind. In a different life, with a different upbringing, and someone to bankroll my dreams, I would have started my own catering company. I chose the safe route and went with accounting instead. Ann says it's never too late. Here, in her lovely kitchen, I can see what she means. It makes me think of the renovations Chet is doing to mine, and I realize all hope is not lost. False starts are a part of life.

Meanwhile, she wastes no time kicking off her heels, asking me to do the same, moving into full-on work mode. She's throwing orders left and right and I can't seem to get a word in edgewise. It's too bad because a part of me wants to tell her all about Chet. I want her to notice how good sex looks on me. I want her to notice that I'm different. I'm desirable.

But apparently there isn't time for that. Apparently, everything is about her list of preparations that is miles long.

I shouldn't be surprised. The neighbors are right. Ann takes entertaining to another level. Everything she does is on another level and as much as I hate to admit it, I can appreciate that. They say you rise or fall to the level of those around you. I believe it.

In any case, at least the busy work helps to take my mind off of the things I'd rather not think about. It helps me avoid the impending disaster in my own home, and I mean that literally and figuratively.

I like my handyman well enough. He fucks me good. And I won't lie. There's a part of me that revels in the fact that my husband is essentially paying him by the hour to do it.

But it would be unwise not to give things room to breathe.

"Thank you for this," Ann tells me earnestly. "I'm so grateful you could help."

"It's no problem," I tell her. "That's what friends do."

"You're sure?" she asks, fishing. Maybe I was wrong. Maybe she is more perceptive than I thought.

"I'm sure," I say, because she doesn't know how good I, too, can be at withholding. My dream of being an event planner, avoiding Chet, and my goodwill are not the only reasons I agreed. I've started to notice that the other women in the neighborhood are dropping by Ann's place with greater frequency. It stings just a little to see another car in her drive or someone else sitting on her front porch. It's crazy. I know it's crazy. But how are you meant to concentrate on fixing all of your problems? How are you meant to live your life with this sort of shit going down?

I have no idea. I only know that every time I see her with someone else, I can't help but wish it were me.

"We have one goal tonight," she tells me as she lays out more cocktail napkins and lines them up with surgical precision. Once.

Twice. Three times, she checks her accuracy. "We need to make sure everyone drinks up."

"I don't foresee that being a problem," I say watching her as she makes her way around the kitchen. There's something in the way she moves. She moves with the kind of grace and confidence I wish I had, almost like she was given the extra dose the rest of the world was shorted. When Ann is satisfied with the placement of her monogrammed napkins, she moves on. But not before turning toward me to give me the once-over. I smile. *You're right, Ann. Something is different.* "What's up with you today?"

"Nothing."

Her face falls. She's disappointed by my lies. "This is serious, Sadie. I want everyone happy tonight—everyone needs to have a good time."

"I understand."

This time it isn't just her expression that changes, her entire demeanor shifts. She doesn't like it that she can't figure me out, that she can't pin me down. She turns away again. But she's not fooling me. She's going to come at me from another angle. "Paul's home, and I want to make tonight good for him. Darcy will be here too. There's a lot riding on this party. "

My bottom lip juts out. Not that she's looking. How sweet that her words carry daggers. It's almost like she's trying to make me jealous. It works.

"Anyway—there's more champagne out in the garage. Just make sure we don't run out and keep everyone's glasses filled. God knows they need it."

I don't offer a response. I'm too busy filling champagne flute after champagne flute in preparation for her guests' arrival. *Any moment now*, I think, checking the time on my phone. I'm secretly hoping to see a text from Ethan. But I suppose Chet would be a halfway decent substitute.

"Do your arms hurt?" Ann asks watching me put the phone away and then stretch my triceps. Always one to look on the bright side, she's reminding me in her subtle way that not only am I kissing someone's ass, I'm getting a workout in at the same time. "Here," she says. "Let me."

She runs her hands down the length of my arms and back up. It doesn't go unnoticed when I get the chills. "Better?"

"Yes."

"Have a drink. It'll help warm you."

"I'm not so sure."

"Well, I am. Have you seen the people in this town lately?" she asks. "They're like zombies. They could stand to loosen up a little."

I don't know what she's getting at. I can't help but take it personally. "Who specifically?"

Ann cocks her head. "Do I really need to answer that?"

I wouldn't have asked otherwise. I shake my head. I know better than to say what's on my mind.

"God," she says. "I don't know why I'm so nervous. But I am. I just want everyone to be happy, you know. It's the holidays."

I recall my husband's favorite words. They work on anybody. "Don't worry. I'll take care of it," I tell her, even though I don't really know what exactly *it* is.

"You promise?"

"I promise," I say, making a mental note to stay away from the champagne. Then, when Ann is once again preoccupied with her list, I pop an Ativan for good measure. It should help with my clammy palms and the flip-flop feeling in my stomach.

"So...." Ann says, handing me veggies to chop. I brace myself for what comes next. I can tell by her inquisitive tone that she knows. I'm pretty sure she can smell sex and happiness on me. She clears her throat. "What's your New Year's resolution?"

I pretend to mull her question over as I slice cucumbers and then arrange them on a tray. The chopping goes on and on, and it never ends. I have no idea how many people the Bankses are expecting, but apparently it is a lot. Finally, I tell her, "I don't do New Year's resolutions."

"What a shame."

Once I've finished arranging the last of the vegetables on the tray, I move to the other side of the kitchen where I can stare down the lane toward home. It feels like waking up after a long slumber. Ann asks who I'm looking for. *What* I'm looking for. This is her way. As much as I enjoy her company, she has a way of going too deep, too fast. I think that's what Ethan liked so much about her. *You should check out her podcast. She's real. She doesn't hide behind things. She tells it like it is. I think she could help you...*

Ann picks up the knife I used for chopping and tosses it in the sink. "I feel like you're missing a major opportunity for hope—for growth."

"Probably."

She walks over to where I'm standing. She twirls me around, forcing me to face her. "I know the holidays are hard. God, do I know. But you can't lose focus, Sadie. You can't. And it would serve you immensely not to be so cold."

"I'm not."

She gives me that "atta girl" look, the one we all crave. "Fine then. What's the one thing—out of anything—that if you could have it—you'd want?"

"I—"

"Let that be your resolution."

Obviously, Ethan comes to mind. "People always want what they can't have."

"No," she tells me. "People always want what they *think* they can't have. It's about what you want to believe, Sadie." She says it so flippantly, like she doesn't know the pain of rejection, of losing something she really loved. "Now, what is it that you *really* want?"

"I don't know," I say.

She looks me up and down. "I think you do."

"My husband," I confess. "I'd like to have Ethan back." I'm not expecting to blurt it out the way I do. It's been ages since I've said his name out loud. So long, in fact, that it feels foreign and forbidden on my tongue.

"Ethan," she repeats, searching my eyes.

"Yes, Ethan." His name comes out like a thought that has been stuck way down deep inside that has somehow been dislodged. I can see that she doesn't believe me. I can also see that she's confused. I can see that she was expecting something different. She doesn't want to let her disappointment show.

"And you're prepared to do whatever it takes?"

"I think so."

"Then you shall have him." The way she speaks with such ease, it gets me. It's so easy for her, too, the way she works me over. It surprises even me that at the slightest hint of another person's touch, I give in, offering up my secrets like a gift.

Suddenly, Ann swallows hard. Something in her expression shifts, and a decision is made. "I wish I could tell you how many things I almost let myself believe impossible before they were done. Turns out, few things really are."

"Like what?"

Unfortunately, she chooses not to elaborate. "Getting what you want is not rocket science, Sadie. Just a set of very specific measures one has to take."

With a slight shake of my head, I agree to something unspoken. It isn't hard to do. I don't think another person has or will ever look at me as intensely as she is right here and now. Her conviction makes me want to believe. Somehow, she has enough for the both of us.

CHAPTER TWENTY-SIX

SADIE

"I'm glad we could get away for a moment," she says as we schlep champagne bottles between the detached garage and the house. "There's something I need your assistance with…"

Ann speaks in code, so it's hard to ever know what she really means, even when you think you do. "What?"

Once we've dropped the bottles off in the kitchen, she takes my hand and leads me back to the garage. She closes the door behind her, but this time she doesn't flip on the light. Moonlight floods in via the skylight, and slowly, as my eyes adjust, I can see that she is patting one of the built-in countertops. "Can you hop up here for me? I have a surprise for you."

Following a shrug, I hoist myself onto the counter. Ann leans forward, trapping me, resting the weight of her body on her hands. "I realize," she says with a touch of sorrow, "That this is very, very inappropriate."

"Ann—" I make a move to get back on solid footing.

"Shhh." She parts my legs with one hand, and holds me in place with the other. When she thinks she has me where she wants me, her fingers find their way up my dress. "I love this on you," she says and suddenly, the dress that was meant to be returned to the store has become my most valuable possession. "Do you like me, Sadie?"

I shrug in the darkness. "Sure."

"No, I mean do you *really* like me?" she asks, her fingernails sliding so slowly upward and then back down again. The truth is, I haven't made up my mind. I *think* I like her. I'm just not sure I like her in the way she means at this very moment. I've never been into women. To be honest, I've never really been into anyone other than Ethan. Aside from Chet that is—and him—I'm just using to fill the void my husband left. But I don't say any of this, of course. "Yes."

"Good. I want you to be happy, Sadie."

My throat is tight; I can't breathe. My body responds to her touch, even if my mind isn't sure. Something deep in the pit of my stomach aches, leaving little doubt that I'm in deep. "I am happy," I lie. I lie because you can't feel this many feelings about a person and be happy, really. If I know anything, I know that falling in love is perplexing and lovely and confusing and captivating. It's the most marvelous thing that can happen in life. And also, the worst.

"I'm sorry," she tells me, burying her face in my lap, the warmth of her breath heavy against my thighs. "But sometimes…I meet someone…and sometimes I can't help myself. This is one of those times."

Her words make me feel weightless. They're breathtaking and wonderful and hard to believe. It's astonishing that someone like Ann Banks could want someone like me. It's flattering, to say the least. So much so, that I forget to ask myself what my motivations are. I'm too filled with bewilderment. She looks up and takes notice. Ann is careful, controlled, and quite possibly everything I've ever wanted to be myself.

"If what you want is your husband back, I have a little secret to let you in on…"

"What's that?"

"You have to make him jealous. Like I said, men are very simple. They want to conquer. You have to show them you're something worth conquering."

"How do I do that?"

"You're doing just fine I'd say."

"Ann—"

She searches my eyes and gives me a wry smile. "Here, let me show you."

"Ann—"

She presses her hand over my mouth. She shushes me and then she wastes no time. She goes straight for my panties—she slips one finger through them, she goes for the kill.

My heart races so I know I'm not dead. I could be close. Ann says you should always begin with the end in mind, and that's where mine goes. But I do not ask her to stop. "Oh good," she says, her eyes flicking upward toward mine. "Just what I was hoping for. I'm sorry. I hope you don't mind. It's just…I can't help myself."

She slides one finger inside me and then another, until I realize she's wrong. She is helping herself, and me too. My head lulls backward, and I'm staring at the ceiling, but I see nothing. Nothing at all. Ann works her magic, and before I know it I'm coming; this is so wrong, but nothing has ever felt more right.

Just when I think she's never going to stop and that I might never ask her to, she does. She removes her fingers and I watch as she pops them in her mouth. "For so long, Sadie," she says, "I've been waiting to taste you."

"You've only known me for a few weeks."

"And I've shown incredible restraint waiting that long."

She perches on her tippy toes and kisses the corner of my mouth. She tastes like me. "And *that* Sadie is how you seduce a person. You just take what you want. You render them defenseless, just as I've done here."

I exhale long and slow.

"Oh, and before I forget," she says matter-of-factly then kissing me full on. She bites my lip softly, and this makes absolutely no sense, but I hope there's more where that came from. Her expression turns serious. "I need the scoop on Luke White...anything you know...anything you can offer. I mean, I realize teachers hear things..."

With the tilt of my head I ask, "Darcy's son, Luke?"

She nods. "That's the one."

"I'm just a sub...and I haven't even been there much lately."

"Hmmm."

"Why?"

"Ugh. I don't know what to do—but it has to be something. The little bastard is teasing Neil."

"Neil?"

"Yeah—in the locker room—last week—Luke took his shoes and put them in the toilet—then he hid his clothes so he had to wear his sweaty gym uniform the rest of the day."

"Jesus," I say. "Kids these days..."

She takes my hand and helps me off the counter. "Yeah. And I've tried to talk to Darcy about it."

"How'd that go?"

She gives me a look. "About like you can imagine. Can you believe she just turned it all back on Neil? Suggested he must have done something to deserve it?"

I actually can believe it, but I don't say this.

"I'll see what I can find out."

Ann smiles. "Thanks, Sadie. I'd really owe you one."

CHAPTER TWENTY-SEVEN

SADIE

The night rolls on, and I do my best to put what happened in the garage out of my mind. It isn't easy. I'm distracted. It doesn't help that Ann avoids me. Whatever bliss I felt earlier turns first to unease and then quickly to regret. Ann is a good friend. Now is not the time to ruin that—or to make things awkward. By the same token, she is also not the kind of woman one rejects and lives to tell about it.

"I want you to pass these out," Ann says, sneaking up behind me. "To the women."

"What about Darcy?" I ask my eyes searching the crowd. "Does she get one?" I want her to know that I understand her, but once again she proves how hard it is to ever really know a person.

She kind of scoffs at a very reasonable question. "We aren't in high school, Sadie. Everyone gets one."

I don't say anything because what is there to say when someone calls you out for being juvenile? Before I can think of anything else, Amelia comes bounding down the stairs, headphones covering her ears, two friends trailing behind. I look over at Ann, wondering if she is disappointed in me. Maybe she wanted more reciprocation in the garage. Maybe I should say something about it. It's hard to know with her. One second she's into to me—she's telling me she can't help herself—and the next she's biting my head off. Whatever the case, obviously she has a short fuse, and I'm learning how important it is to stay clear of the trip-wire.

But now, standing beside me, she doesn't look bothered. To the contrary. There is such a look of satisfaction upon her face that a lump forms in my throat. That's the thing about letting go of a dream—it has its way of resurrecting itself, of sneaking up on you in the most obscure ways. And sneak up on me it does.

Suddenly, I am thinking about how I'll never have that—how I'll never ever know what it feels like to have something—anyone—to make me that happy. Something, or rather *someone* that really belongs to me. Forever. Not just pretend forever, either, based upon some made-up, shaky vows. Something that is mine and mine alone. Something that could never be taken from me. Something that could never leave, even when it does, because we are tied together in ways that nothing could ever change.

"Excuse me," Ann says looking over at me. "I need to have a word with my daughter."

I don't bother with a response. I'm too preoccupied over-thinking the rest of my life. Maybe that's why I don't notice that someone is standing behind me until I am startled by his voice. "Teenagers," he remarks. "Can't live with them, can't live without them."

When I turn, I see that it's Paul, Ann's husband. Interestingly enough, we haven't officially met. I mean, I've seen him here and there. But he isn't home much, and unlike his wife, he tends to shy away from the spotlight. I offer a closed smile.

"I'm sorry," he says, taking a step forward so that we're shoulder to shoulder. "I didn't mean to scare you." He turns and extends his hand. "I'm Paul."

"Sadie," I offer. "From down the street."

"Yes, I know. I've heard quite a lot about you."

Funny, I think. I've heard almost nothing about him. Ann really only talks about her husband in an abstract sort of way. But he isn't abstract. He's right here in the flesh, and he's handsome—though surprisingly short—and charming, and everything I imagined him to be. It's easy to see what she sees in him. It's all there in his reserved nature. "Ann told me about your situation," he adds, and his demeanor shifts to one of uncertainty. "That was thoughtless of me, the remark about teenagers."

I look at him blankly. I have no idea what she has told him of my situation, only that it sounds bleaker than I'm pretty sure I've ever let on. "It's fine."

"Ann says you're subbing at the high school."

"Yes."

"She's really fond of you, you know. My wife."

"Really?" I smile. Then I get an itchy feeling in the back of my throat. It goes by the name of guilt.

"And you should know…Ann doesn't feel that way about many people."

"Well," I say, glancing around their living room. "People certainly seem to be fond of her."

"That's the thing, Sadie. People are always fond of a party." He sips his champagne slowly and gazes over the crowd. He has a presence about him, the kind that causes you to watch from the corner of your eye because you just can't help yourself. "It's the clean-up crew who deserve the real credit though, isn't it? Those that get in there and get their hands dirty."

"Yes," I manage. *He knows what happened in the garage.* Or at least, he suspects. Did Ann tell him? Or is he as perceptive as his lovely wife? Either way, I make a note to stay to help out afterward. Right from the beginning, the Bankses never did make a point explicitly.

"I just hope you won't let her down," he says and it's clear what's happened. Ann is using me. And oddly enough, I don't mind at all.

"I'll do my best."

"Good," he says. "Because she really needs this. And quite frankly, I really need her to be happy."

I smile, nod, and down the rest of my drink.

I DON'T WANT TO LET ANN DOWN, AND I WANT TO GET AWAY FROM Paul, so I deftly hand out the invitations as she's asked. By the time I make it 'round to Darcy White, she along with Ann and a few other women I don't know have isolated themselves to a corner in the Bankses' library. It doesn't make any sense, now that I've gotten a better look at the room, why Ann's favorite book is on the bookshelf under the stairs instead of tucked away in here where it could be safe.

I'm thinking so hard about this, and about what happened in the garage, and what Ann's husband said, that I forget I am standing side by side with strangers. I stare too long at the books. I forget to listen to the conversation and to laugh and nod in all the right places. This is what I mean when I say I am not good with people. Books, I can understand. They give up their secrets, eventually. They say what they mean. People rarely do.

Ann leans in and asks me if everything is all right. Her fingertips brush mine. It feels like electricity, a current that is moving too fast. Everything is, in fact, not all right. I want to ask her about what Paul meant when he said she needs this. *He couldn't possibly have meant me, could he?*

But I can't ask her now. Not with everyone around. I've just realized I'll have to develop sharp elbows if I want to get any time alone with her. These women are like vultures, and they're circling, circling, circling. Mouths move, but I don't hear anything that is being said. A shrill sound plays in my head, reverberating around, until it's sharp and relentless. Ann asks me again if I'm okay. Nothing feels okay, but I nod, because people never really say what they mean or mean what they say. I nod because I've spotted her first book, the one that Ethan tried to gift to me, and now I am once again thinking too much and thinking leads to bad places.

It leads to places like me wondering who is using who. It leads me to ask myself how I really feel about Ann making me come. It makes me wonder where Ethan is and whether he's alone. *Is he thinking of me? Will he text?* It leads to me think about Chet and where things stand between us. *How long do I have to keep this going before Ethan catches wind of it?*

This leads me to check my phone. I know Ann hates this. But I can't help myself. It is only when I go to retrieve it from my pocket that I feel the lone invitation still in my hand. I hand it to Darcy. I practically throw it at her, to tell the truth. "It's an invitation," I say, because she looks confused. Her expression quickly turns to one of pity as she takes it from my hand. "Thanks," she tells me. "But I'm really quite busy."

The room goes quiet, and everyone is waiting for me to respond but my mouth is too dry and my eyes dart toward Ann's book. *This will help you,* I hear Ethan say. *You can make friends. You can be normal again. You can be like you used to be.*

I think what he really meant was: *this is how you let me go.* Darcy's words sting, but Ethan's cut like a razor blade and they're all colliding with one another. In my mind I picture myself grabbing them in midair, catching them in my fist and squeezing, squeezing until they've lost their power. I imagine telling Darcy what I really think. But everyone is watching and waiting, and if I say what's really on my mind, it will not end well.

Ann takes me by the arm. "Excuse us," she says, pulling me out into the hall. Her head is cocked and her gaze is transfixed. She leans in and whispers, "What is with you?"

"Nothing. I'm just tired."

"I need you Sadie. God, I want you. I want you so much."

I don't know how to be needed, so my response is stupid and off topic. "Paul knows."

Her expression doesn't change, so I say the next most stupid thing. "I don't know what's keeping Darcy so busy...all I ever see her doing is gardening."

For a second Ann seems surprised. She recovers quickly. "Let me guess...in nonexistent shorts and a low-cut top?"

"Yes," I tell her. I have no idea how she knows this. Summer is long gone, and Ann didn't live on Penny Lane then. "I swear she used to flirt with Ethan."

She offers a tight smile. It fades fast, though, and then she shakes her head. Her eyes dart toward my shoes. If I didn't know better, I'd say she almost looks hurt. "It's not polite to gossip."

A sort of apology rises to my lips. But before it can find its way out Ann says, "Oh, Sadie. Don't acquiesce for the likes of Darcy White."

DARCY WHITE'S BODY WAS DISCOVERED AT THE BOTTOM OF THE pool at approximately 1:31 a.m. It was too cold for a swim. It appeared she took one anyway.

CHAPTER TWENTY-EIGHT

HER

She didn't have to make things so difficult. It's not as easy as it looks, holding a person underwater. Easier than smothering them on land—sure. Still, I suppose of all the ways to kill someone, it's the least labor intensive. Unless, of course, the water is cold. Trust me—then it's pure hell.

CHAPTER TWENTY-NINE

SADIE

A person typically drowns in less than a minute. It doesn't look like it does on TV. Ann knows this, so I know this.

While distress and panic may sometimes take place beforehand, drowning itself is quick and often silent. A person close to the point of drowning is unable to keep their mouth above water long enough to breathe properly and therefore is unable to shout. Lacking oxygen, their body cannot perform the voluntary efforts involved in waving or seeking attention.

The instinctive drowning response is the final set of autonomic reactions in the 20 to 60 seconds before the victim sinks fully underwater. Uncontrollable movement of the arms and legs, rarely out of the water. Eyes glassy and empty, unable to focus. Head low in the water, mouth at water level. Head tilted back with mouth open. To the untrained eye these reflexes can look similar to normal, calm behavior.

In emergency situations, it is advisable to wait for the victim to stop moving or sink before approaching, rescuing, or resuscitating. While the instinctive reaction to drowning is taking place, the victim will latch onto any nearby solid objects in an attempt to get air, which can result in the drowning of a would-be rescuer as well as (or instead of) the original victim.

Ann knows this, so I know this.

Not that anyone was watching. No one saw Darcy go in the water. Her friends say she seemed fine, and her husband swears she wasn't drunk. For several weeks afterward, neighbors speculate on what could have happened. *Had she drank too much? Had she meant to do herself harm? Had someone wanted her dead?*

Ann certainly disliked her, and she had been capable of bumping a cyclist with her car, and possibly causing a man to fall from his ladder, but is she really capable of drowning a friend?

I don't know. And more importantly, if I did, could I prove it? Should I tell someone, and if so, would they think I was making it all up? It's all so confusing.

Ethan always told me I care too much about things that don't matter. He liked to throw around words like "obsessive" and "neurotic."

I realize he is probably right when Ann says, "I'm sorry that she's dead. But perhaps what really gets me about the whole things is, who is going to remember her, Sadie?"

Everything about her conveys exasperation, so I tell her I don't know. She looks tired today, as much as a woman like Ann can. It's a lot to have a dead body so close to home. Or so I presume.

She hasn't mentioned what happened between us in the garage, and she hasn't made another move. Ann projects. She channels her energy into worry over other things, instead of what's really bothering her. She expresses her anxiety in her work, in meddling in her children's problems, in asking questions no one can really answer. She's different in real life than who she portrays herself to be on the internet. She doesn't let her problems go to waste. She milks them.

My mother was like that. Growing up, we didn't have much. That's how I know that I haven't yet hit rock bottom. I've seen worse. We were poor. Dirt poor. Irrevocably poor. In turn, mother made sure to never let a thing go to waste. If she cooked a chicken, she'd find a way to use it all. In the same way, I watched her work herself to death until she was all used up. Minus the financially challenged part, Ann is like that. She asks the question again, hoping it will change something. "Outside of her family, who is going to remember Darcy?"

"*Really.* I don't know."

"Paul has spoken with the family, and they agreed to donate some of the organs that could be salvaged."

"Salvaged?"

"Organs need oxygen to survive, Sadie. Darcy drowned," she says as though I'm unaware. "The water was cold. So there's that."

"What does that mean?"

Ann gives me the side eye. "It means there are a few things they can work with."

"Like what?"

"Bone, liver, corneas…skin."

My mind can go a lot of places, I'll admit. But it never, not even once, went there. I don't know what to say. Ann is expanding my life. She is very informed about a lot of things, and I don't want to seem unintelligent by asking too many questions. Now is not the time to say the wrong thing. Not when she's in this kind of mood. "Well, at least some good is going to come of it."

"A lot of good, Sadie. A lot of good. You have no idea."

I can only shrug. Ann has a way of making a good point.

CHAPTER THIRTY

SADIE

A death in the community really shakes things up. For Ann and I, Darcy's untimely departure certainly has that effect. She goes radio silent on me. She gets busy. As usual, some places inside of her are easy to reach. But others are encrypted, grueling to decode.

Paul comes home for a week, and Ann says they need time. I worry that she's using this as an excuse to avoid me. Maybe she's changed her mind. Maybe she's had enough of me. She wouldn't be the first person. If anything, I've learned when you think you know what you're dealing with, you usually don't.

Still, Ann assures me everything is fine, she says time is important in a marriage. She says it's all you have.

It certainly feels like all I have. I go to DUI class, I come home. Chet waits. Chet works. Chet and I have sex. Chet leaves and I'm thankful for another day to slow his progress. I lay in bed and toss and turn. I don't sleep. Eventually, the sun rises. Chet comes back. I do it all again. Lather, rinse, repeat. This is my life.

I can sense the world is going on without me. It feels like I'm sleepwalking through this one and precious life. All the while, Ann is slipping away. My home is slipping away. My marriage is slipping away. My bank account is dwindling. I'm about to be homeless. There aren't many subbing gigs to be had lately, which is a real bummer because I need the money in a bad way. Even if it isn't much.

Maybe this is rock bottom, I think as I lie there each night. By dawn, I'm certain. It has to be.

∼

THANKFULLY, NEAR THE END OF THE WEEK, I FINALLY GET A CALL. Strep has hit the campus, and they need me to sub. Sometimes you realize you're just one unfortunate circumstance away from better luck. Relief floods over me. Sometimes what feels like rock bottom is maybe just a blip.

There's only one problem. I've only made it halfway down the driveway before I'm forced to come to a full stop.

Ann is pacing back and forth across my drive.

She's like an apparition. It doesn't make any sense. It's pouring rain out—it's the kind of day I would have just as soon preferred to stay in bed. But not Ann. I note her running clothes. They're new. I note the way they hug her body. Jealousy washes over me like rain. If only she didn't have to be so hardcore. She never misses a run, not even for rain, apparently not even for time with Paul.

It's not just her attire that is seductive. She wears a Cheshire Cat grin, as though I've been caught doing something interesting, when really I'm just going to work.

She waves and I ease up on the brake, roll backward a little, and let down my window. Ann rests her hands on the door and leans in. "Where are you off to?"

"They called me to sub."

"Oh," she huffs, glancing toward the house. After a few seconds she backs away from the car. She folds over to rest her hands on her knees. She's panting hard. When she speaks, it's forced out in bursts. "Speaking of…I'm glad I caught you. I wanted to ask…"

I wait and wait and wait. Rain trickles in.

When she finally looks up, her brow is knitted. "Have you noticed anything strange with Amelia?"

"Amelia?" I shake my head. "No. Why?"

"Who's been picking her up after school?"

My heart picks up pace. "I'm not really sure. Subbing is still slow. Today is the first time I've gotten a call in forever."

Ann has the icy look down to an art. She offers it so freely now.

"What? They haven't really needed me."

"Before that."

I pretend to mull it over. "I couldn't say. I'm in the classroom. Mostly."

"But you've seen her, right?"

"It's a huge campus."

"Still, you must have seen her…she hasn't been riding the bus. As a matter of fact—I'm pretty sure she's been lying to me for weeks."

"Oh…"

Ann rolls her neck, and then arches her back in full stretch before resting her hands on her hips. I mustn't forget, she's trained at spotting liars, trained at sussing out the details she wants. "Who was she with, Sadie? When you saw her?"

I want no part of this conversation. It's not the time, and even if it were, I'm in a hurry. Even I know enough to know that delivering bad news about someone's kid is akin to telling them their spouse is having an affair. It never turns out well for the whistleblower. "Umm…the girls from the party…I think."

It's hard to tell a lie if you aren't sure.

"Kendall and Elea?"

I shrug. "I don't know their names."

Unfazed by the fact that the rain has picked up, Ann whips her phone out, scrolls a bit and then holds it up to my face. "Is this who you saw her with?"

I squint at the screen. "Yeah, the girls from the party."

"Anyone else?"

"Not that I've seen. But like I said, I haven't been there."

"Okay." It's as though she is speaking more for herself than to me. "That's good."

"Why?"

"No reason. I'm sure it's nothing."

I check the time on the dash. "I have to go."

She rests her hip against the car door as though she doesn't plan on going anywhere anytime soon. "Call and tell them you can't come in after all. I have plans for us."

"I just told them I'm on my way."

"So. Call and say your car won't start."

"I can't do that."

"Sure you can." She backs away, slowly at first, before coming at me full force. I can only watch as she leans her skinny little frame through the window and reaches all the way down until her fingertips brush the lever to the hood. Somehow she manages to pull it, and then she is walking around the car and I am following, and she is disconnecting my battery wire.

I should stop her. I should say something. But what? Considering that whatever I might say could land me in the hospital with broken limbs tomorrow or worse, six feet under? It's not like I'm afraid, anyway. Curious, more than anything. She's got me where she wants me, hanging by a thread.

"See?" she says, brushing her hands together. "Easy peasy."

"Ann…I have to go."

She shrugs. "You can try to start it if you want…"

"Ann."

"I'll pay you double what they're offering." She orders me to take my phone out. Forces me to hand it over. She dials the school. Hands the phone back to me. Stares me down while I tell them my car in fact won't start. The words come out easier than I expect with her standing there. It helps, she says, that it isn't a lie.

"Now," she says motioning at me once I've ended the call. "Now, we get to it."

All I can do is stare. I've never met anyone like her, and it has just occurred to me that I probably never will again. She shakes her head in disbelief. "Are you excited?" she demands. "You don't look excited."

"I'm—"

"Whatever. It doesn't matter. We have a lot of work to do." She starts down the lane toward her house.

I slam the hood and then follow. "What kind of work?"

Ann doesn't answer me at first. In fact, I'm pretty sure she picks up pace. "So. Much. Work," she says. I realize my questions are pointless. I realize what Ann wants, Ann gets.

Ann knows this, so I know this.

ANN LEADS ME INTO HER HOME, INTO HER OFFICE, INTO THE BELLY of her life. She pulls out a chair, motions for me to sit and then she situates another chair so that she's facing me, our knees nearly touching. "We've been intimate," she says. "And, now, I would like to take things one step further. I think it's time."

My eyes widen.

She leans forward slightly. I'm thinking I haven't yet had enough coffee to make for a satisfying sexual encounter, but I'm willing to give it a shot when Ann says, "I need to know that I can trust you, Sadie. I need to know that you want this too."

How can I say this? It would be a big, fat lie. I don't know what I want. My whole life is up in the air. This doesn't stop me from nodding anyway and telling her she can trust me.

"I'm not going to lie to you," Ann tells me. "You are not the first woman I have loved."

My teeth grind together. Whatever it takes to keep a straight face. "But I'm really hoping you can be the last."

"Me too," I say and it isn't a lie. It's cold-hearted, unfortunate truth. To imagine her saying these words to anyone else, to imagine anyone else getting this close to her makes me feel a little bit sick.

Ann smiles. She leans forward and kisses me hard and rough, and then she pulls away and tells me there's more where that came from, but first, we have to change lives. She places a phone in my hand. She tells me she needs help on the suicide line.

She gives me instructions on what to do. She says to keep the caller talking. She gives me a list of questions to ask. Name, age, occupation...lifestyle questions. She says not to worry about remembering all of the answers. She says the calls are recorded because it's important to listen between the lines. We practice on each other, each of us taking turns being the one who wants to end it all. She says I'll sound more natural if it doesn't sound like I'm reading from a script. She says it's what sets her hotline apart from all of the official ones. I don't ask what she means. There isn't time. The phone rings. And it rings and it rings.

CHAPTER THIRTY-ONE

SADIE

Everything has a solution, Ann says. She is busy working on a new book. My morning hours are filled with the hotline so that she has time to put words on the page. She says she needs to focus, that a first draft requires all of her, and that she's sorry, but by afternoon, there isn't much left of her to give. It's mostly okay. I have Chet for the afternoon. He's always happy to take a break. Eagerly, he fills my evening hours too.

He's working on the master bathroom, and we've hit the shower and managed all of the counters. I'm careful not to let him fuck me in the bed. There's something too permanent in that. It feels like third base, when I prefer to stay safely on first.

I probably have nothing to worry about. He hasn't tried to tell me his story yet. He could have a wife at home and a house full of kids for all I know. Not that I care. He's a welcome distraction. Nothing more. Nothing less.

Still, in the haze of sex, he whispers that I'm beautiful. I wonder if he knows that appearances can be just as deceiving as words. Chet doesn't know me. Not the way he thinks he does

Speaking of appearances—in front of our neighbors, Ann blames her recent obscurity on her devastation over Darcy, like everyone. She keeps to herself mostly, and when she doesn't, she speaks in hushed tones and lowered glances. But with investigators, I notice Ann is different. In the few times they've stopped by while she was writing and I was running the hotline, I notice she's curt. She conveys a clipped and factual manner, and quite frankly to me, she seems put off by the whole thing.

"What can you do? " she asks one afternoon as we shop for patio furniture. Never mind that patio furniture is next to impossible to find in January. Even in Texas. Ann says nothing is impossible, and all life is eternal. The heart wants what the heart wants. She said that to me specifically about Ethan. Don't be dense, Sadie, she'd remarked earnestly. Of course you can't just let go. Love never dies.

More often than I care to admit, I find myself appreciating Ann's perpetually sunny nature. Somehow, she has an answer for everything. No problem is insurmountable—even our neighbor's death. Ann says she wants to help by offering the neighbors grief counseling. And even though I worry the investigators will find out she's doing it, on a suspended license, Ann says everything will be okay because when she gets to the bottom of what really happened, they will turn the other cheek. *No one cares how they come by the information,* she says. Just so long as they have it.

"We're all going to die eventually, Sadie," she's telling me now. "I just wish Darcy White had chosen somewhere else, you know?"

"Me too."

It's like she isn't even listening, because she says, "What happened, happened. We can't change that. We can only use it to our advantage."

I don't see what she is getting at. I don't see what is advantageous about a woman at the bottom of your pool. Messy business, if you ask me. But then I think of my mother. I think of all those chickens, and how she used them up. I consider that I, too, could become like her—used up and discarded. For that reason, I go fishing anyway. "How?"

"It's a long story."

I shrug, because we're looking for invisible furniture, and literally all we have is time. A story could help to take my mind off of things. Shopping makes me itchy. I feel nauseous. I don't see the point, I say to Ann. Why not just order online from the comfort of her own home and not have to see or talk to anyone?

How else am I supposed to show you off, she asks, and suddenly I don't care if we ever find furniture.

She's right. People stare at us, and I tell myself it's Ann's celebrity and not the fact they're wondering what she's doing with someone like me. One person after another approaches and asks to take a selfie. At this rate, I'll never get alone time with her. I take back what I said before. It feels like we're destined to spend an eternity in this store, and all the gawking, doesn't make me feel special. It makes me feel like a caged animal. Worse, Ann introduces me to her fans as her assistant, if she does so at all. Several of her admirers have mentioned how lucky I am. I should be proud. She has proven her point. And yet, that's not how I feel at all. Rage builds threatening to spill out.

"What's with you?" Ann demands to know.

"Nothing," I tell her.

"The dinner is coming up. We should start thinking about the menu."

"Huh?" I feel like I've missed something. Ethan always accuses me of not listening, of zoning out, of being in my own little world. Or at least he used to. She was supposed to dig. She was supposed to call my bluff. She wasn't supposed to sweep my feelings under the rug. Ann is the most emotionally intelligent person I know. This isn't an accident.

"The invitations you handed out...on New Year's Eve. They were for the dinner we're hosting next week."

I like the way she says *we*. I'm aware she's probably referring to Paul but pretending works just as well. I like the way she takes me high and then low. Low and then high. I'm falling in love with her unpredictability, in the way I wish my husband could have fallen in love with mine.

"I thought you might have canceled, considering..."

"No. I think we should do it in Darcy's honor."

"I thought you didn't even like Darcy."

"I liked Darcy fine," Ann snaps. Her eyes dart around the store, and I realize I've spoken louder than I thought. Social cues are not my strong suit. It's apparent in the way she leans toward me and says in the barest of whispers, "You really shouldn't speak ill of the dead, Sadie. And anyway, it's not for us. It's for *them*."

"Them?"

"Yeah. The other women—they aren't like you and me, Sadie. They aren't strong."

I have no idea what gives her the notion I'm strong, but it feels good that someone thinks as much. I'm certainly not going to correct her. Besides, Ann isn't fond of being made to feel wrong, so I throw in a sort of half-laugh. "I know. It doesn't make any sense."

"A dinner party?"

"No, how they can't move on."

"We all need to move on, Sadie. I think we can both agree on that."

Obviously, she means me, and obviously she is referring to my marriage. It would hurt if I didn't have a plan to rectify it.

Ann is aces at social cues. She reads me well. "Don't be so sensitive," she says, and I have to look away. Ethan used to call me that.

I check the suicide phone, annoyed that it's so quiet. Ann insists that we take the phones everywhere. Just in case. Now, I'm glad I have it, and now I'm willing it to ring. Sometimes you just need to know someone out there has it worse than you.

"Come on," she tells me, taking my hand. "Since we can't find furniture, we might as well do something to make ourselves feel better."

"Like what?" I ask, saying a silent prayer she isn't going to force me into another box store. I hope she'll suggest lunch. I'm starving.

Her face brightens. "Something crazy."

I have no idea what crazy truly means to Ann. But as long as it isn't shopping, I want to. I really, really want to. Also, she seems happy again, and she isn't thinking about patio furniture or draining her pool or the police. Which is probably why it doesn't occur to me to question what she has in mind.

CHAPTER THIRTY-TWO

SADIE

Ann goes through my refrigerator first. "There's nothing alive in here."

"I eat out, mostly."

Inevitably, she finds my stash of Oreos and potato chips. And then, she finds the back-up stash, the one I'd kept hidden from Ethan, back when keeping things hidden still mattered. I look on helplessly as she opens the trashcan and flings my favorite things in. "If you want to win your man back—hell if you want to win *any* man," she says. "I'm afraid you have a long way to go, Sadie. This stuff is poison. Absolute poison."

I stare at the floor. It has just hit me. I have fallen for the female version of my husband. Even so, I have to admit, she is at least partly right. I do have a long way to go. A person has to burn about 3,500 calories to lose one pound of fat. I'd need to burn at least 87,500 calories to reach a healthy weight.

Ann knows this, so I know this.

"We have three hours before your hair appointment."

I look at her like she's crazy. "I told you before. I can't afford your hair person."

"Consider it a favor."

"I don't need favors..."

"Don't be obtuse, Sadie. Everyone needs favors. And anyway, remember? I owe you."

"Not *that* much."

"Are you kidding? You've done so much. You helped with Neil. You saved me with the appetizer fiasco. And that isn't even the half of it."

"I can manage this on my own..." I say. "I mean...I'm sure you have a million other more important things you could be doing... isn't Paul home?"

With the flick of her wrist she is waving me off, she is calling my bluff, and I already know what a bloody disaster this is going to be. "Paul is busy. Bless his heart. He works so hard. He lost three patients last week. I think he needs time..."

She closes the pantry door and moves on to the freezer.

"Really," I promise. "We don't have to do this. We could do something—"

"You scratch my back. I scratch yours."

"Ann."

She looks back at me and winks. "Like I said—it's a favor, Sadie. Isn't that what friends are for?"

I don't answer. I can see this isn't going to end well, because the thing about favors is eventually you have to pay them back.

～

"DON'T WORRY," SHE TELLS ME, POINTING AT THE FOOD THAT IS MY lifeline until I find real work. "We're going to clear all of this out. And then I'm going to give you a diet plan and a grocery list."

"You don't have to do that," I say cautiously. "I can manage. In fact, I've been meaning to—"

"No." The tone she uses with me is rough and abrupt and suddenly, I'm thinking of all of the fun things we could be doing instead. "I'm not here to hold your hand, Sadie. I'm not going to give in to what you *think* you want. I'm going to give you what you need."

What I *need* is to get her out of my house.

What I needed was a friend like her. Six months ago.

What I need are her fingers inside of me, her mouth on mine.

What I need is to stop caring what she thinks.

"You have to see how far you've sunk Sadie. If you don't know where you are, how will you ever find your way out?"

I fold my arms and push my feelings down. If she weren't here, I'd eat them. Now, I can only think about eating her. Anything to shut her up. And these thoughts are worse, worse than the cookies, and the chips, and the ice cream combined. "I don't know what you want me to say."

"I want to teach you how to make people do what you want them to do. But first, you have to become someone worthy of influence."

I want her to teach me this too. I just want her to teach me without so many words. Finally, I think all of my dreams are going to come true when Ann crosses the kitchen and takes my hands in hers. "You have to show people your best side and your best side only. Do you know what that means?"

I'm not sure I do, which must be why she bends a little at the knees so we're eye to eye. She stares, she searches, she probes. I've had pap smears that were more enjoyable. "Now, you probably think I'm calling you fat. But I'm not. I'm just saying there's room for improvement."

First, my eyes register vacant surprise, and then my brow rises in astonishment. I don't know what I expected her to say. But it wasn't that.

She squeezes my hands. Harder this time than before. "You remember that woman at the coffee shop?"

It takes me a second, because my thoughts are running around my head a thousand miles a minute. "The cheater?"

"That's right," she nods. "The cheater."

I sigh. I was afraid she might play it this way. She feels guilty. Or she wants me to. But that particular emotion isn't in my limited repertoire. "Essentially," she says, "You're no better than her. Only instead of cheating someone else, it's worse," she says. "You're cheating yourself."

My head cocks. I back away from her. She isn't who I thought she was. Or rather, maybe, I'm afraid she is.

She's saying the opposite of everything she's supposed to be saying, and it's like we're in some parallel universe where all of life is inverted. "That's harsh."

"Life is harsh, Sadie."

"And you know what else? I bet when that woman came out empty-handed to find that she couldn't easily get away after being stood up...I bet she felt at least a hint of shame about what she was doing. To have to explain your tires being slashed in a parking lot—well, it makes you think, doesn't it?

I look away. I roll my eyes. If this is what having an affair with a woman is like, count me out. This is more bullshit than I can take in a day.

"Well, I bet it made her husband think. Why would a person do such a thing? But you see, Sadie, she knows why— and I bet you it will make her think twice the next time she tries to sleep with someone else's man."

I don't say anything. Although, when she asks me to look at her, I do. I want to tell her people aren't property. You can't own a person. But I know this isn't true.

Ann takes my chin in her hand. Her eyes search my face for understanding. "The next time you decide to eat shit—or let yourself go—you'll think about this moment, Sadie."

She isn't wrong.

"And with any luck— maybe— just maybe— you'll make a different choice. The truth is," she says, earnestly, "I can't see myself with you...intimately...not with you like this. Not unless we make some changes."

Tears fill my eyes. But not for the reason she thinks. She isn't telling me she hasn't made another move toward me because of Paul or because she's worried about messing up our friendship. She's saying it's because of the way I look. I'm momentarily relieved. Fat is far easier to get rid of than a husband.

At the same time, she's made another thing clear. I've been a fool. Ann is a liar. She wasn't avoiding me because she was busy. Or preoccupied with her book. Or because of Paul. She was avoiding me to prevent the inevitable letdown on my part. She was avoiding me because she only finds certain aspects of me attractive. The parts that benefit her.

"What's this?" she asks. There's an edge in her voice that gets my attention. In her hand she's holding the paperwork I'm supposed to get signed at DUI education class. Before I can stop her, she's reading it aloud. "I asked you a question," she says when she's finished reading. "What is this?"

"A mistake."

"Driving under the influence?" She shakes her head slowly. Then she closes her eyes for what feels like a very long time. "Really, Sadie? Please tell me I'm imagining this. Tell me this is not happening."

"It's—"

She paces the length of my not-good-enough kitchen with my not-good-enough food while analyzing my not-good-enough life. "I thought more of you than that..."

"I know—"

"And worse—you kept it from me. I've been a complete fool.

That makes two of us.

"I thought we were friends—I got you a job at my children's school, for God's sake. I hired you to help people in my business! I fell for you, Sadie."

"I'm sorry."

"Sorry." Her eyeballs nearly pop out of her very pretty head.

And I realize this was the wrong thing to say. "Sorry? Really. That's all you've got?"

I shrug and try again. I realize how inexperienced I am. If only someone had warned me. Fighting with a woman is so much more treacherous than fighting with a man. One has to employ every weapon in their arsenal. You can't just skate by on sex appeal alone. "I should have told you."

"Damn right you should have. Here I am trying to help you, and you haven't even been honest with me. What do you think people are going to say when they find out?"

What I'm about to tell her is going to make everything so much worse, and still, I can't stop myself. "I'm pretty sure they know."

This does it. Red flushes her cheeks. Ann waves the form violently. "How could you? You let me believe you were some-thing—something that clearly you are not."

"It's really not what you think."

She braces herself against my kitchen counter and hangs her head, and maybe this is what winning looks like. "I let myself care about you...I vouched for you!"

"It was just a misunderstanding," I promise. "I'm not an addict."

She motions toward the trashcan, which has been filled to the brim with the things I'm not supposed to want to eat. She draws her claws and bares her teeth. "Could have fooled me."

I watch her carefully as she takes a deep breath in and holds it. It's amazing how one breath can last an eon. Finally, she says, "And I'm disappointed to say you did."

The realization only skims the surface. The rest will come later. I've ruined things with her. Same as I did with Ethan. Which is a real problem, because it takes two players to finish a game. Solitaire this is not.

Before I can come up with a proper response, she storms out. When she leaves, she takes the last of my dignity with her.

CHAPTER THIRTY-THREE

SADIE

The fight with Ann helps me lose five pounds in three days. The fact that she threw out all of the food in my house didn't hurt.

Nevertheless, time has a way of making you see things clearly. *Should I have told her about my past, about the DUI charge, about... other things?* Maybe. Do I regret my decisions? Not in the least. We are more alike than we are different, the two of us.

What has transpired would not have happened if she knew the real me. Now, she thinks she does. How can a person regret a thing like that? Clarity is a fine gift.

Maybe it was inevitable, maybe it would have happened anyway. But the day I finally decide I've had enough—enough moping around—the day I decide to get up off of the couch and take the steps that Ann says in her book will change my life— is the day Ethan calls.

He wants to know if he can drop by later in the week to grab a few more of his things. He doesn't mention the renovations or bring up putting the house on the market or say which things it is he wants. I know his short-term rental is fairly compact, but it doesn't matter. I'm already convinced his visit is contrived. My suspicion is further confirmed when he tells me how good it is to hear my voice.

It's fine if he drops by, I say. It is his house, after all.

It isn't until after we hang up that I realize his visit will mean missing Ann's dinner party, and that I'll have to reach out and let her know. Truthfully, I'm not sure she wants to see me anyway. We haven't spoken since she walked out, and I didn't want to be the first person to break the silence. So, Ethan's call is timely. I'm not ready to face her, and now I have the perfect excuse. One she'll like. I can tell his name makes her crazy.

If only she knew what a big fan he is.

When I text her, she rings me back immediately. "Call him back," she tells me before I've even had a chance to say hello. "Do not change your plans for him."

The way she says it, the way she speaks, it is as though nothing has happened between us. Partly, this is a welcome relief, like salve to a burn. Grace incarnate. Actually, hearing her voice feels like the first time I can truly breathe in days. I need her. And here she is, offended on my behalf and offering advice. This means that she still cares, and if she still cares, there is hope. "If I do that—he'll come by when I'm not there."

"So?"

"So, I want to see him."

Her voice lowers. "This is what you do. Are you listening?"

"I'm listening."

"Turn off the automatic garage opener. Lock the dead bolt and exit through the garage."

"Yeah, but then how will I get in?"

"Simple. Leave a window open. He won't know that, and when he asks, just mention you had to step out. Say you're sorry you forgot about the lock—but now that you're living alone, you're taking a little extra precaution."

I can't help but smile. Ann always thinks of everything. Life is so simple for her. The rest of us just miss the obvious. Little does she know I have claws too and I'm sharpening them by the minute. "But I want to see him."

"I'm sure you do. But you, Sadie, you are not the kind of woman who breaks plans for a man."

I consider what she is saying. For a second, I think about contradicting her. I want to tell her I am exactly the kind of woman who breaks plans for a man. I am the kind of woman who revolves her whole life around said man. But I don't say any of this. I still want to win. "You're right."

"Repeat after me," she says. "I am not the kind of woman who breaks plans for a man."

"I am not the kind of woman who breaks plans for a man."

"Perfect," she tells me, and I swear I hear her clap her hands in the background.

CHAPTER THIRTY-FOUR

SADIE

There are fifteen of us in attendance. Paul is out of town again; it was a last minute thing. Transplants almost always are, Ann says.

She seems disappointed, although, I can tell she's trying not to let it show. I feel the same way. I feel myself being drawn to her bay window where I can get a glimpse down the street at my house and with any luck, at Ethan's car.

Ann's three-course dinner, however, does not disappoint. Everyone agrees—even me, who hardly ate any of it. I could feel Ann's eyes on me, warning me. I was not to enjoy the butternut squash ravioli she served as an appetizer with the rosemary browned butter, not even the salad with the baby kale, Asian pear grapes, candied walnuts and gorgonzola honey vinaigrette. I pick at the lamb chops, barely. But the honey yogurt panna cotta with the blood orange sauce is totally off limits.

I am aware I am being punished. It comes in many forms. Love is wise to the wounds upon which to press. Nothing tastes as good as skinny feels, Ann whispers to me.

I beg to differ. But then, it's been a long time since I could pass for what's considered skinny.

Eventually I can't take it anymore, so I excuse myself to use the powder room. I check my phone for any missed messages. Naturally, there aren't any. So, I have to give myself a bit of a pep talk before going back out to the party. I pop an extra Ativan to see me through.

As I round the corner, toward the kitchen, I run into Amy. Literally. The hall is dark, and I'm not expecting her to be there. She knocks the wind out of me, forcing an audible gasp. She reaches out and grabs my forearm to steady me. "Sorry," she whispers. "Are you okay? I thought you saw me."

"I'm fine," I say rubbing the spot where our heads bumped. I scoot to the side to allow her room to pass, but she doesn't move. "Actually," she tells me, her voice strained, "I was looking for you."

"Well, you found me."

She leans closer and lowers her voice. "I was just wondering…" she starts to say before she trips over her words. "Have you noticed…"

She tests my patience. My head throbs. I help her out. "Have I noticed what?"

"Well," she says hesitantly. "I was wondering if you've noticed anything odd about Ann?"

"Ann?"

"Yeah…I can't put my finger on it, but something seems off."

"I hadn't noticed. No."

She leans into the wall. "I'm sure I'm just being silly…it's just, I know you two are close, and well, I was just looking for—"

"What were you looking for?" Ann asks, appearing like a magician. It's her specialty.

"The ladies' room,'" Amy says nervously, the way you do when you're caught red-handed talking about someone behind their back.

"It's there," Ann points. No one says another word. Not even me, who realizes there's truth in Amy's question. I have noticed something about Ann. She hasn't invited me here because all is forgiven. She invited me here to keep an eye on me. Same as Darcy.

～

LATER, AFTER THE TABLE HAS BEEN CLEARED, AND THE WOMEN HAVE cordoned themselves off in the kitchen, Ann clinks a knife against a glass to gather everyone's attention. "I'm so glad we could all get together," she says. "Especially in light of what happened." Slowly, she dries her hands on a dishtowel. God, I love her. Her hands especially. "It's important to be there for one another."

Most of us nod our agreement.

Amy, Darlene, Kathryn, Lisa, Heloise, and Denise do, anyway.

Personally, I'm not so sure. I just want her alone.

Either way, the result is the same. She keeps talking. She keeps stalling what is inevitable. "We should do this more often," she suggests. "Make it a regular thing."

"That's a great idea," Lisa says.

Ann smiles. "I think we should make it official."

"Like a club?" Denise asks.

Once again, Ann is all smiles. "Like an alliance."

"This isn't one of those multilevel marketing deals is it?" Kathryn jokes. "Where you're going to try and recruit us..."

"No," Ann asserts. She has that devil-may-care look when she says it. But I can tell she means business. "This is something to make our lives more fulfilling."

"Those lamb chops were certainly fulfilling." Kathryn laughs.

Ann ignores the lame attempt at humor. "I've seen the way you ladies look forward to my parties. And there will definitely be more where that is concerned—but—I don't know...I want more. And—correct me if I'm wrong," she says, glancing around the group, from woman to woman. But never at me. "I think we all do."

A couple of them shrug. Some glance at the person standing

next to them. No one knows what to say, so just like in the rest of their lives, they look to someone else from whom to take a cue.

Ann goes on. She may be addressing us all, but she's really only speaking to me. "No one looks up from their phones these days. Everyone's reality is based on somewhere they aren't. We have friends, sure. But how many of them do we actually ever spend time with?"

"Not many," Heloise admits.

"Who has the time?" Amy wants to know.

Ann presses her lips to one another and hesitates momentarily before continuing. I love her speech. It all seems so well thought out, so well rehearsed. "Well, I'll tell you who doesn't have the time, and that's Darcy."

Suddenly, everyone is staring at Ann's Brazilian Spruce flooring. Everyone except her. And, me, of course. We've all heard the story of its import, and how lucky they were to find that much in the exact color of cherry they desired.

"Maybe Darcy was depressed—I don't know."

There's a rumbling of agreement.

"The truth is—none of us know what happened that night—or at any time previously. And that's what bothers me most. We were supposed to be her friends."

"She seemed distracted at the party," Amy says. "I could tell something was bothering her. And she mentioned once that someone—that another mom at the school—had been harassing her."

"Harassing her how?" Kathryn asks.

"She wouldn't say," Amy tells us. "But I told the police."

"What did they say?" I can't help but ask. I'm careful not to look in Ann's direction, although I'm dying to see her expression.

Amy shrugs. "They didn't seem to make too much of it."

"We should have been there for her," Darlene says like a confession.

"Let this be a lesson," Ann says. "We can do better. We *have* to do better."

"I thought she was happy. She seemed happy," Heloise offers.

No one looks up from the floor this time. Not even me.

"How about you Darlene?" Ann asks. "Would you say you're happy?"

I watch as Darlene shifts her weight from foot to foot. I know her truth better than anyone. She lives directly next door. My days are long and boring, and I had time to observe her in action. Or rather, they used to be, but people don't change that quickly. "*Happy?* Define happy."

"I mean, are you fulfilled in your life? Does it have meaning?"

Darlene's discomfort at being put on the spot is palpable. "I don't know...I guess."

"Who *is* happy?" Lisa demands coming to her aid.

"I am," Ann says. "And I want that for you too."

"What exactly is it that you are suggesting?" Kathryn chimes in, and God, I wish she'd shut it. She doesn't realize how abrasive her tone is. Ann hates that. I worry for her.

"There are women, women in this kitchen, women in this very room, who are going through things," Ann says to Kathryn and everyone. "Some who have done things, things they aren't proud of."

"What kind of things?" Amy wants to know.

Ann sighs long and heavy and slow. She leaves room for them to draw their own conclusions before offering an answer. "Terrible things."

The women inhale as a collective. Ann's breathing remains steady. The stage is set. All eyes are on her. "But we can help them. Because if we've learned anything from losing Darcy, we've learned that helping others helps us all."

CHAPTER THIRTY-FIVE

SADIE

A few weeks after the dinner party, Ann shows up on my doorstep late one night out of the blue. "I'm sorry," she says. I haven't even gotten the door all the way open before she's brushing past me. She's wide-eyed and scary and fascinating all at once. "It's just that I have to go out of town, and this can't wait."

"Is everything okay?"

"No, Sadie. Everything is not okay."

"What is it?"

"Something is going on with Amelia."

My stomach lurches forward into the future without me. "What?"

"I don't know," she says, answering none of my questions. "But it's bad. I have a feeling it's *really*, really bad. I caught her sneaking out of the house. Not only that—she's been lying to me—I think she's seeing someone. Someone she knows I won't like."

"How do you know?"

Her eyes narrow. "Call it mother's intuition."

"I—"

"Anyway," she says, cutting me off. "I need you to keep an eye on her while I'm away."

"Of course."

"I have to know I can trust you. This is the most important thing I've ever asked anyone."

"Of course you can trust me." She looks me up and down like she's trying to determine whether I'm telling the truth. "Where are you going?"

"Another author canceled on *Good Morning America*. My publisher thinks it's a good idea to send me in her place."

She crosses my living room and takes a seat on my sofa. She places her head in her hands. "This time of year is very popular for self improvement. They've decided to send me on a seven-city tour following the show. They want me in several targeted territories. Basically, where the action is."

"That's great!" *This is the worst thing that's ever happened.*

"It's not great. In fact, it's the last thing I need."

"I see."

"You don't see, Sadie." She crosses her legs. "This is the worst possible time. My kids need me here. *Paul* needs me here."

I don't know what to say to her. Sometimes there is nothing to say.

"I know things have been shaky between us. And I'm sorry for my part in that. But I wouldn't ask if it weren't important. I need you to promise to keep an eye on things, Amelia in particular. She's at such an impossible age. Promise me."

"Okay, I promise."

She bites her lip. "You'll call or text me for anything?" she asks. I've never heard this much desperation in her voice.

"Of course."

She exhales swiftly. I can see a weight is lifted in the way she almost smiles. "Oh, Sadie. You can't know how much this means to me. I love you. I really love you."

I say, "I know." And then, because I know it matters, I ask. "What are you going to do? About Amelia?"

She shakes her head. "I don't know. I just have to trust that it will take care of itself."

~

IT'S LONELY AND QUIET WITHOUT ANN AROUND. I WATCH HER ON *Good Morning America*. Sometimes we touch our own wounds to be punished. I know because the ticker scrolling across the bottom of the screen reads: "She's like your best friend, but better. The toughest asset you'll ever have. Meet Ann Banks: America's newest guru." Her stint goes so well there are other shows after that. Everywhere, she says, they are trying to book her. Her trip gets extended.

We keep up mostly through text. Although, even those are different. Her messages are short and clipped. I wake up angry and go to bed that way too. I don't like sharing her with all those people, and all they print are lies.

Paul has to go out of town on business. Ann warned me this might happen. She says this is for the best, but I know it's not, because the kids are basically raising themselves. The truth is, I'm pissed at her for choosing work over her marriage, over her children, over me.

To make matters worse, the hotline is busy. It never stops. Ann says I am doing a good job. She says you can only do what you can do. She says everything works out in the end.

But I know that's wrong, because the vet called again this morning. The grocery store kitten is beyond ready to go to the shelter. I've been avoiding their calls for days and days—maybe even weeks now. I figure they're still charging me to keep her, so, so what? Anyway, the latest voicemail was adamant. They can't keep her there. Fueled by rage and a touch of loneliness, I don't even have to pop an anti-anxiety pill to make the trip. I literally, aside from fielding endless calls from desperate and hopeless people, have nothing better to do.

Thankfully, this visit to the vet proves itself to be more pleasant than the last. Everyone is so nice. So nice. They were even kind enough to add a pet carrier to my bill. After I sign the bill authorizing the transaction for thousands of dollars, the technician brings her out. He says, "I'm sorry about before. When I treated you poorly."

Just kidding. In my imagination, that's what he says. In reality, he tells me, "We've been calling her Little Annie."

Of course you have.

The girl behind the counter giggles. "You know, like Orphan Annie?"

"Yeah," I say. "I get it."

It's amazing how things can shift in such a short time. Ann says in her book it's important when we're down that we move up the emotional scale. Rage is one step above anger, and that emotion is one I can access easily. Maybe longing isn't so far off.

The technician hands me the carrier, and I peer in. The same small eyes, although they are bigger now, stare back. A paw reaches out and swipes at my finger. Her claws snag my skin, drawing blood. It's a welcome feeling.

"She's quite playful," he tells me. "A real hunter."

No doubt.

"Cats are great companions," he says. "She'll make someone a good pet."

"Just not me," I say. "My husband is allergic."

"That's too bad."

It is. It really, really is.

Finally, he gives me directions to the shelter, although I've already looked them up. Little Annie cries nonstop all the way there. In the lot, I allow myself one last look. "I hope you're grateful," I tell her. "I hope you get a good home."

She yawns big and wide and then she stands, like she's ready to pounce, like she wants to play. Like I'm prey. She rubs the side of her body along the carrier door, begging to be petted, so I stick my finger through the metal grating. Her fur reminds me of Ethan's hair.

My eyes water. And I don't think it's allergies.

"He's not coming back," I say.

She answers by swatting at my finger with her paw and then leans forward, biting at the tip playfully. Her teeth are small and sharp and they hurt. She draws blood. I don't know what changes in that moment, except that I recall something Ann said the other night at the dinner party. *If you're going to suffer, it's better not to do it alone.*

So what if Ethan hates cats? That doesn't mean I have to. He may be allergic. But I'm not. Maybe what you think you want isn't what you need. And maybe what you need isn't always what you want.

Like Chet. Like Ann. Like this cat. Maybe life is twisted and mixed up that way.

"It's settled," I say to Little Annie. "Looks like you're coming home with me."

CHAPTER THIRTY-SIX

SADIE

There comes a point in every person's life where they can no longer lie to themselves. For me, this is that point.

It started out as a game, but it didn't end that way. Early on, not long after we were married, not long after we'd moved to Penny Lane, I picked up the wrong toothpaste at the grocery store. It was the first and the last time. "What's this?" Ethan asked, bringing me the box.

"Toothpaste."

"I can see that. It's not my brand."

I squinted at the box and said, "You'll live."

"That's the wrong thing to say." He pressed me backward against the kitchen counter cornering me with his body. "I'm afraid you're going to have to pay for this."

I smiled and then wiggled away. I wasn't in the mood for sex. At the same time, I was also aware that I couldn't say no again. It would be the third consecutive refusal, and I was pretty sure my husband was counting. He usually did.

"Bend over," he ordered. At first I thought he was joking. It wasn't until he took me by the hair and used more force than I could resist that I realized he wasn't. It wasn't until he pushed my pajama bottoms to the floor and spanked me— once, twice, three times—that I realized it was downhill from there and not in a good way. Later that night, long after my husband had drifted off to sleep, as I surveyed the damage, the broken blood vessels in my back side, the tears in my vagina I didn't have to see to know they were there, I realized there was no coming back from this. I could have sustained a lot of forms of humiliation. An affair, ridicule, the silent treatment. But this kind, I wasn't sure about.

THE FOLLOWING MORNING HE WOKE ME BY BRINGING BREAKFAST TO bed. For a moment, I thought I'd dreamed what had happened. Ethan had never been abusive. We dated for a while before getting married, and so long as I'd known him, our sex life had always been fairly conventional. "I can tell you liked our little game," he said, kissing my cheek, and I realized denial wasn't going to be an option.

"Actually—I didn't like it."

He searched my face. "Ah," he laughed. "See, now I don't know whether or not I can believe you."

"You hurt me." I showed him the bruises. "It's not really my thing."

"Huh…" he murmured, scratching his chin. "Because you seemed really into it."

I pushed the tray away. "I wasn't."

He slid it back in my direction. "Relax. Geez…I was just trying to spice things up a little."

"Like I said, it's not me."

"Exactly. And that's the beauty of it. Sometimes," he smiled. "When two people, are married, when you've been together as long as we have—well, sometimes you want something different."

"I don't think the something you want," I said, "is me."

He shook his head and stood abruptly, causing the tray to tip. "I think," he replied. "I think in time you'll find that it is."

I cleaned up the mess, and I said nothing. I suppose I should have seen it coming. But I didn't. I really didn't.

$$\sim$$

THE GAME THAT DIDN'T FEEL LIKE A GAME AT ALL CONTINUED. Ethan assured me rape fantasies were normal. He said he'd spoken with a therapist, and that these fantasies helped to get out his aggression. He said that she explained that desire and love are not mutually exclusive, and that sometimes what turns you on intimately is very different than what you actually want or do in real life. He explained that fantasy was just that. He said acting them out would help our marriage. He hadn't meant to hurt me. He was just excited, and he took it too far. He promised to be more careful in the future. He said marriage was accepting all of a person, not just the parts you liked.

But mostly, he didn't talk about it. He just found new and unusual ways to surprise me. Our *game*, as he liked to call it, often started with any perceived infraction. Like a charge on the credit card he hadn't approved of. Or a towel being folded improperly. Or my growing refusal to want to leave the house.

The final straw was the night he bailed me out of jail for the DUI. I knew what was coming. I knew he wanted to play his game, and that's why I left. Perhaps subconsciously, I was looking for a reason not to go back. Maybe jail seemed like as good an alternative as any.

After we got home, he tried his usual tactics. He accused me of upping the ante. First, there was the cornering. Next, came the hand covering my mouth. Then, his belt wrapped around my throat. He liked to pull tight as he forced himself into me.

"I'm your husband," he said when I pulled the knife on him.

"And if you ever touch me again," I told him earnestly, "You'll be my dead husband."

Even still, he thought it was a part of the game. And maybe it was.

I stabbed him in the thigh anyway.

"You're going to regret this," he assured me as he packed his bags, his wound leaving a trail of blood along our creamy white carpet. I didn't. I only regretted the choice in color. "You're going to come to realize I am the only person who has ever really loved you."

The unfortunate thing about that is he was right —my husband did love me. He *does* love me.

And I love him.

He has his flaws. A big one, to be sure. But time has a way of clouding even the worst of things. And, well, desperation has a way of seeking its own level, the same as water.

If only love had an on and off switch. It doesn't, and it's possible to love a person, even if they do terrible things to you.

Obviously, for my husband's fantasy to work, I had to play the part. I couldn't let him think I enjoyed what he was doing to me. An actor is never to let the mask slip, so long as the audience is watching. That's a sure way to paper cut their attention. Real life and magic cannot coexist. At some point, we all have to make a choice.

I don't know what he expected me to do with the knife that night. I only knew that the stakes had to go higher and higher, otherwise the fantasy could not continue. Like a fire without air, it would be extinguished.

I hadn't thought that forcing him from our home would cause him to lose interest. I hadn't yet realized that our marriage was like a scab he couldn't help but pick. He'd already made up his mind about wanting out, and maybe he saw an opportunity, an easy out, and he took it. He didn't stop there. Not my husband. Nope. He picked and he picked and he picked.

I only intended to up the ante. Make the game more exciting. For a little while, it almost did. Until it didn't.

I hadn't foreseen that he would seek easier prey, a.k.a. the neighbor girl. *The neighbor girl.*

That's where he went with it. So, I did too. In a different sort of way. He needs something to punish me for? Fine. Because I've spoken with a therapist as well. We've become very close, and she assures me that marriage is about meeting the other person's needs. Which is why, this round, I've gone all in.

CHAPTER THIRTY-SEVEN

SADIE

One afternoon, as Chet and I are rebuilding my fence, Ann appears at the edge of my yard. "What on earth?" she asks surveying the mess.

"You're back," I say.

Her head cocks, and her brow furrows making it clear that she has worked out in her mind what is going on. If she has this reaction, I can't imagine the one my husband will have. "This feels like a party I wasn't invited to."

I smile. The satisfaction of surprising her gives me great joy. Plus, smiling is easier than telling the truth: working alongside Chet was better than hanging out alone. Nailing boards into place seemed like it might be therapeutic. I'd filed for a divorce that morning, thereby initiating the final round of our game. If the vet bill hadn't done the job, no doubt asking for half of his wealth would.

"IT FEELS LIKE WE HAVEN'T HAD A PROPER CONVERSATION IN

forever…it looks like you've been busy while I was away," she says to me the following morning over coffee.

"Not really."

She glares at me over her mug. "You got a pet, remodeled half of your home, lost a bit of weight…"

I can't help but smile at the fact that she noticed. She's right. I have slimmed down, and I'm about to be nearly one hundred and sixty pounds lighter, a bit of information I intend on saving for the right time.

"But I asked you to keep an eye on things, Sadie."

"I did."

"That's not entirely true though, is it?"

"What do you mean?"

She licks her lips, and it makes me think of the other pussy in my life. Cunning and calculated. "You broke a promise."

"Everything was fine," I assure her. "Amelia was home when she was supposed to be. I called the landline, like you said."

"Did you watch her though? *Really* watch her?"

"Well—no—but—"

"It's fine," Ann says cutting me off. "Like I said, you were busy."

I tear a piece off of the Danish she has shoved in my direction. She tells me to eat, so I do. The last thing I want is to further offend her.

"You have to be careful around your handyman," she says, refilling my coffee, baring her teeth. "You'll never win Ethan back if you get yourself tangled up in that mess."

"He's nice."

"I can see that." She sits down on the barstool next to me. Her eyes search mine. "I also saw the way he looks at you—the way you flirt with him. Seems a bit more than nice if you ask me."

"It's nothing," I say. "Just friendly banter."

"Just friendly banter can be trouble, Sadie." She hops off of the barstool and strides across the kitchen. "Which would be a shame.

You're doing so well, losing weight, getting on your feet. The last thing you need right now is a complication..."

"I—"

She shakes her head. "Don't argue. What you're doing is trouble, and you know it. What you're doing is—playing with fire. I just hope you don't come crying to me when you get burned."

"We're just friends that's all."

"No, Sadie," she hisses. "You aren't friends. He's your employee."

"Well, technically he's my husband's employee."

"Exactly—and don't you think he might be feeding information back to his boss?"

"I don't think—"

"That's right, Sadie. You don't think. That's why you have me."

I swallow hard. I force more coffee down to avoid saying the wrong thing again.

"Well, on the bright side," she exclaims. "It's not like Ethan's filed for divorce yet. So he obviously doesn't know."

This makes me smile. Tightly. Smugly.

Her brow rises, a look of warning is offered. "Just be careful."

I decide not to tell her about the divorce. If she still has hope—better to let her have it. I can't bring myself to extinguish that.

IF ANN HAD HER SUSPICIONS ABOUT WHY ETHAN WAS HAVING WORK done on the house before, she never said anything. I'd planned to tell her the truth. I just needed time to let it settle within myself. To say something out loud has a way of making it real. I wasn't sure if I was ready to make the end of us real.

Had Ethan not shifted all of the money that was left in our joint account, I wouldn't have. I fired a warning shot off the bow with the vet bill. He decided to go to war. He was angry—angry about the money—angry about me stabbing him. Angry about me changing the locks. Angry about a lot of things. Problem was, he couldn't show up to show me just how angry, on account of the cat. Allergies are killer that way.

If he wanted to act out his fantasies, he'd have to level up.

More than anything, I realized, he was angry that he'd forgotten how to win at his own game. I was calling him to be more. Only he'd missed all the signs, and my more competitive side reveled in that.

TWO DAYS AFTER SHE RETURNED HOME, ANN TEXTED, AND ASKED ME to come down and help her with the hotline.

To be honest, I wanted to say no. I could just as easily field calls from the comfort of my own home. But the messy truth is, I missed her.

I'm afraid that we are living on borrowed time, the two of us so, how could I not agree to her request for help?

Let yourself in, she texted. *I'll be in my office.*

I did as she asked, and I did find that she was in her office. But then, so was my handyman. Neither one of them were dressed, and they were doing what Ann said was trouble.

CHAPTER THIRTY-EIGHT

SADIE

"I know you're angry at me," Ann says when she phones later that evening. "But it's not like I meant for it to happen."

"What about Paul?" I ask, a question that has been weighing on my mind, really, more than any other. "I thought the two of you were happy..."

"Of course we're happy."

"Then why would you—"

"I did this for you, Sadie."

"For me?"

"Yes, for you. You get yourself tangled up in these situations, and sometimes it's like I just can't get through to you."

"I don't know what you're talking about—"

"Look," she interrupts. Her voice is cold, but the bite is almost gone. "You think you know things, but there are a lot of things you can't know."

I don't have a proper response for her. I'm too irate. I can't see straight, much less possibly formulate coherent thoughts and turn them into words that she will understand. What she has done is unforgivable. And worse, she dragged Chet into the mix.

"Anyway," she says like a confession. "I didn't want this to happen."

"But it did happen."

"Oh, Sadie, love. This is what you should know about liars, cheats, and deceivers: It's easy for someone to show up in your life and tell you that they love you; it's much more difficult for them to demonstrate that love consistently. That's why Chet couldn't say no to me. He doesn't love you. Which means he isn't worth your time."

"It wasn't about love."

"That's where you're fooling yourself. Everything is."

I hear someone speaking to her in the background. She places her hand over the speaker, then I get muted. When she comes back on the line, her tone has gone from indignant to sanguine. "Anyway, even you can't turn a blind eye to what this means. It's opened a door for us; we've turned a corner. I know your secrets — and now you know one of mine."

"One of them?"

"Everyone has secrets, darling. You know that. Although, that's not why I called. I have a favor to ask of you."

She is impetuous, and I am half in love with her, and so I say the only thing in the world that makes any sense. "What?"

"We'll discuss that later," she says quickly. "I just wanted to know you're not terribly mad."

"I'm fine."

"You're not fine. But you will be. Soon enough you'll see that this was for the best. One day down the line, when you and Ethan have reconciled, you'll understand. Sometimes you have to tear things down before you can rebuild them."

"We—" I try to tell her that I filed for divorce. I try to tell her that she's just fucked up the one bright spot I had in my life. But as usual, she cuts me off before I get the chance.

"We can't let a man come between us, Sadie. Not now. Not ever."

I don't say anything. What would be the point? She's already won so completely.

"Oh and Sadie," she whispers into the receiver. "That handyman of yours…let me tell you, he knows a thing or two about tearing things down and rebuilding. God, I wish you'd told me sooner. He is amazing in the sack."

ANN FINDS HER WAY INTO MY BEDROOM. THE CLOCK BESIDE MY BED reads 12:43 a.m. She climbs under the covers and slips her hand up my T-shirt. I ask her helplessly how she got in. She says she ripped the key off of Chet, of course. She tells me she's very resourceful. But she proves it when she twists her fist in my hair and kisses me on the mouth. Hard and relentless, desperate and seeking. At first, I tell her no, but I wasn't sleeping anyway and I suppose what she's come for is better than lying there bored.

She heads south and I let her do what she does, not only because she does it well, but because she owes me after what she did with Chet. She whispers her secrets into the darkness and my thighs. We make love, and I don't say no to that either, because she's offering a kindness I want to take.

I don't say no, because every love affair has its rituals. And because if she stops her brand of sorcery, I just might kill her for what she's done, and like Ethan says, this is the kind of sex I like. He says it's the only way I know how to connect. My husband is right. I know this because afterward, Ann orders me to get dressed. She says she has something she wants to show me. Something unbelievable.

CHAPTER THIRTY-NINE

HER

I smell blood before I see it. She is asking for you, they tell me. Who they are referring to, I don't yet know. I only know I hate blood, and this feels keenly like my worst nightmare.

Ann told me where we were going. To see Paul at work. I hadn't really thought too far past that, which as it turns out is usually a mistake.

She leads me into an office, and then into an operating room, and the next thing I know I'm inhaling burning flesh.

The room is cold and sterile. About like you might expect. There's music. Classical. It almost, but not quite drowns out the whirling and the buzzing of the machines. I hate surgery, I say to Ann. She smiles and tells me to hold my breath, it'll all be over soon. She reminds me of my mother in that way.

I don't listen about the breath holding, a pity really, because something smells like barbecue and now I realize I'll have to hate barbecue forever. A day will never come again when the smell of it will not remind me of flesh opened up.

But how could I not want to see this for myself, Ann demands, as I hurl into a bag she has shoved into my face. She was asking for you, after all, she says incredulously, and then she tells me it's sort of my fault that she's here.

If I weren't in the process of wrenching up my guts, I would remind her of what she says in her book: Guilt is a useless emotion.

She grins proudly as I wipe the remnants of the contents of my stomach from my mouth with the back of my hand. You're very sexy when you're vulnerable, she tells me, and that's when I hear the small voice. She's there, Ann says. Behind the partition.

"Please," the girl pleads. I step around so that we're face-to-face. Her eyes are wild. "Please don't let them do this."

"It's going to be okay," I say. I don't really know this, of course. But sometimes you have to lie in order to tell a greater truth.

"No," she cries. Her hair is matted. She's put up quite a fight, Ann says. "I'm sorry," the girl says. Her breath is ragged, and her face is as white as the lights shining down on her. "I'm going to die, aren't I?"

"Shhh," I whisper, patting her hand. "Are you in pain?"

She shakes her head from side to side to the extent that she can. "That's good," I tell her as my fingers brush against her restraint. She flinches. It's subtle, but we both notice. I release her hand and walk around the table in order to have a word with Paul, as much as I'd rather not. "What is going on?"

"Come with me," Ann says, and she's whisking me back around to the other side where the patient is crying. "Paul needs to focus."

"I don't want to die," the girl says. I don't tell her she isn't going to die, because the truth is, I don't know. The best I can offer her is a reassuring smile.

"It's funny," Ann says. "All they can think about is dying, and then you get them on the table, and it's the last thing they want."

"Who is she?"

"Kelsey," she replies hollowly. "From the hotline."

I watch as Ann injects more drugs into her IV. Paul leans over the partition and offers a furtive glance, a knowing look. He's good at reading facial expressions and mine asks why she isn't asleep. Mine asks what the hell is going on.

"Why?" the girl manages around sobs. "Why me?"

Ann watches me carefully. She tells me not to worry. She says they always ask these things. "Don't worry," I say to Kelsey. "The doctor is very good. He'll take care of you."

Her eyelids flutter before they close completely. Maybe it's the drugs, maybe it's resignation. Only time will tell. "This is what I had to show you," Ann exclaims. "It's the final secret between us."

I'm not sure I follow. She senses this. "This is the reason for the hotline," she motions toward the girl's head. She's very pretty. Her face is nearly angelic when she isn't crying. "We're traders."

"What's a trader?"

"We give those who want to live the chance."

I know there's more. "And?"

"And the ones who don't—the ones who call seeking a way out —they give their organs."

"What my wife means to say is—we're matchmakers."

"But Kelsey isn't dead."

"She's one of the lucky ones," Ann tells me. "Sometimes, we give repeat callers something to be grateful for."

"Like a new lease on life," Paul interjects.

"Or we help them die," Ann shrugs. "It depends—it's an art— not an exact science."

"It's pretty exact, dear," Paul counters.

They have an entire argument, as Paul cuts and sucks and extracts, about the exactness of medicine in the modern world. It lasts an age, and at the end, even I am not sure who came out victorious. Ann says life is like that. She then goes on to explain how they can't save everyone but they can save someone. Someone, she tells me, who is a fighter, someone who has the will to live.

The girl doesn't speak again. Paul echoes his wife. She's a lucky girl, he assures me. He says he's only taking a kidney. It could have been worse. I'm lucky too, Ann wants me to know. Lucky that it wasn't.

I ask what I'm doing here. I ask her what will happen if the girl talks. She won't, Paul says. He doesn't expand on why, and I don't ask him to.

"You know that old saying?" Ann asks. "You sweat in practice so that you don't bleed in the game? Well, it carries a lot of truth."

A kidney is good for my first assist, Paul says.

It's not as bad as the corneas, Ann says.

Or bone, Paul agrees. Bone is almost as bad as taking a person's eye, he says. Skin is particularly messy. It takes forever.

Lungs are arduous.

Hearts are tricky.

CHAPTER FORTY

SADIE

Ann is just standing there, dropping bombs. Telling me how it all started, telling me how much she is helping people, telling me how much money there is to be made selling organs to those in need. But mostly, she's saying it isn't about that at all.

It's a slow morning for the hotline, something that I now know to be grateful for. Gratitude expands, Ann says, the more you practice it.

Except, I'm kind of not grateful all of a sudden, because Ann keeps talking, and it goes on forever and it never ends.

She's telling me what a relief it is to have everything out in the open. She's saying she's been on the hunt for someone like me, for a partner, for too long. Penny Lane seemed like as good a place as any to find what she was looking for. She's telling me that when we met, she just knew. Right from the start, all of her prayers had been answered.

I was it.

Forever and always.

Her twin flame.

I don't even know what that means. Ethan is my soul mate, and I was under the impression we were only allowed one of those. But maybe I've gotten it wrong. I'd ask—but I know how she gets whenever I bring him up, so, I might as well save it.

Not that I could get a word in, even if I wanted to. Ann is pacing. She's rummaging through drawers. She's flinging things around the room. All the while, her mouth is moving a mile a minute.

It feels a bit strange to see her flying off the handle. Maybe this is her undoing, her unraveling. Maybe I should be concerned. After all, she's entrusting me with so much. Little does she know if she'd just shut up for a second, I have a plot twist of my own.

There's time for that. For now, I'll let her have it. She has come alive under the weight of her words: she's dramatic and wild. She's beautiful and scary; she's unpredictable and precious. As always, everything is about her. And, this moment, this morning, is no different.

She does this sometimes, I've come to realize. Overcompensates. It's the reason for her parties, her over-parenting, and her strange obsession with making sure Paul is incessantly happy. I tell her she needs to slow down, take it easy, and let me help. She says it's nothing—she swears everything is fine—especially now. She assures me that I am helping. But she can't know what I know.

She says it's probably just a touch of resistance over her writing that has her so worked up. It's the new book. There's so much pressure. I can't imagine. "Oh God," she cries. It could be writer's block coming on. Apparently, there are no atheists when it comes to book deadlines.

But I know better.

It's not about the book.

It's not about the organs.

It's not about the pressure.

It's none of those things.

Ann is avoiding the truth. She has elaborate ways of going about it, not unlike the rest of us. Her fans, all the people she is trying to help…she's no different. It's far easier to pick apart other people's inadequacies rather than face your own.

"Look at this place," she says, and believe me, I am looking. Her office is a wreck, not entirely unlike the rest of her life is about to be. Copies of her manuscript, marked up in red ink, are spread out everywhere. There's a method to her madness, she swears. "Oh, Sadie," she cries. "I've got to get myself together. Paul is due home this evening."

"Sit down," I say. "Let me help."

She doesn't budge, and I make a move to start tidying up. But I know better than to touch her work. That, I steer clear of. She's more sensitive about it than most things. Well, most everything aside from what I'm about to bring up.

Momentum is momentum, and once the decision is made, I can't stop myself. After all, as she would tell you, these are the kinds of risks you take when you love a person. When you want the best for them. When you really see them for who they are, not what they want you to see.

When the room is tidy, the only thing left to do is to tackle the bigger mess. "Sit down," I say again. I motion toward the chair I had been sitting in. "There's something I need to tell you."

"It's about Amelia," she says. "Isn't it?"

Ann knows things. She always knows.

"Yes," I admit. "It is."

She doesn't sit. She picks up her manuscript and shuffles it. Then she glares at me. With her eyes. With everything she is. She knows that what I am going to tell her is going to change every-thing. Eventually, she sighs. She goes to the office window and stares out over Penny Lane. "She's sleeping with her math tutor, isn't she?"

"He tutors her?"

"Yes," she tells me. "After school."

I hadn't realized.

"I saw them together," I confess. "I thought you should know."

She says, "I'm going to kill that bastard."

I say, "Let's be rational."

"That is rational. Men like that, Sadie, they never stop."

"So...what? You're going to kill him?"

"Did you ever expect any other outcome?"

"No." *Not really.* "How?"

I wait for her to answer. Instead, she scrolls through her phone. I don't think the answer can be found there, but maybe I am wrong. "I haven't decided yet..."

"What if you didn't?" I say. "What if there were a better way? What if you went to the police?"

"Don't be ridiculous," she snaps. "What good would that do?"

"They'll put him in jail."

"So?"

"So, he'll be punished for what he did."

"Sometimes," Ann tells me, "punishment isn't enough."

I was afraid Ann might do something risky. Something riskier than all of the other things put together. I'd never seen her that upset, or that angry, to tell the truth.

This is why I confronted Ethan at work that afternoon. I knew he wouldn't expect it, not there, and I knew the ball was in my court.

Of course, he denied anything inappropriate was going on. But it was clear in the snow-white color of his face and the stunned look in his eye that he was lying. I told him her parents knew. I told him I was going to the police the following morning if he didn't go directly there himself and confess to engaging in a sexual relationship with a minor.

He looked at me. I could tell he was trying to gauge whether or not I was serious, and I could tell he'd made his decision when he ran his fingers through his hair and swore she said she was eighteen.

Sixteen, I said. She's sixteen.

I'm sorry, he said.

I know, I said. *But not half as sorry as you're going to be.*

Help me, he said.

I smiled and told him I was.

Afterward, I texted Ann and told her what I'd done.

That was brave of you Sadie, she wrote back. *Call you later.*

CHAPTER FORTY-ONE

HER

Of everyone, she means the most to me. My little girl. I can recall vividly the day we brought her home from the hospital. She was so tiny, so wrinkled and pink. She was and still is the most beautiful thing I've ever seen.

I'd hoped she would turn out to be a boy, because a part of me always knew it would come to this. There is only one other person I have ever loved more, and that is her mother. The day she was born was the day I realized an even greater love was possible, and that I would do whatever was in my power to protect it all. Forever.

That tiny thing grew, as tiny things tend to do. As she grew more beautiful and more like her mother by the minute, it crossed my mind that inevitably she would meet a man like him. He was my worst fear materialized.

Unfortunately, I had been too busy to see. But not too busy to know that sooner or later you lose the things you love. I just hadn't thought it would come so soon.

She's not a girl, not yet a woman.

She's not completely innocent. No one is.

I know that.

But there are a few things he should have known.

Like the law.

She's underage.

She's my daughter.

And I protect what's mine.

This is how he ended up drugged, bound, naked, and just alert enough to be afraid. I placed him in his bathtub, where I cut into him slowly. I wasn't precise, the way I am in the operating room. I drew it out slowly, in the way that would make sense if one were attempting to slit their own wrists. All the while, I told him the story of her birth, and how fortuitous it turned out it was the day his death was decided.

CHAPTER FORTY-TWO

SADIE

I didn't see her put my husband in the tiny bathtub of his small rental apartment and slit his wrists that afternoon, but I'm certain she had something to do with it.

Also, she was right. Hearts are tricky. I know because Ann fixes my life, and the next thing I know, she is pushing me to hang myself with a resistance band. In asphyxiation, the most important component between succeeding and failing is the type of knot you use. The figure-eight knot is a good one.

Ann knows this, so I know this.

The biggest drawback to using the figure eight is that it can be extremely hard to untie. But that's irrelevant, and in this case, a complication I won't have to worry about. One more thing to be left for someone else. This, Ann says, is why paramedics carry knives.

If I can't master the figure eight, she says, there's always the bowline. A bowline knot forms a loop on the end of a rope, and the knot tightens further with any increase in pressure. This is why it is useful for hanging things.

Don't stress, Ann says.

There's time to figure it out, Ann says.

She tells me to imagine my funeral and work backward, so we can ensure the right number of people will be in attendance. A funeral is more important than a wedding, Ann says, because unlike marriage, you only get one shot at dying.

So far as we know.

She says it's just a matter of time before the police figure out all of the murders are related. She says every good story must come to an end. She says I am the weak link, and coincidently linked to them all. She says she knows that I wanted Ethan murdered. She says she handles these situations for lots of spouses. It's an easy way to get organs and money, and who cares, because everyone wins.

We go over what to say if and when the police come to my door. She's pissed I hadn't told her about the divorce. She says the cops might point fingers if they suspect his death might not have been entirely self-inflicted. She says I know too much, and she shouldn't have trusted me. This is why if I want to kill myself, she isn't going to stop me. She says she loves me dearly and that she doesn't want me to die. But the alternative, she says, is life in prison, and she would rather see me dead than locked up. She just couldn't bear it.

Prison doesn't make any sense. None of this makes any sense. I was a good person when Ann Banks walked into my life. Maybe I wasn't sleeping much, and maybe I was overeating, and maybe I wasn't taking care of myself. Maybe I was a bit of a mess. But I was comfortable in that mess. I knew I'd find a way out of the fog. Eventually. I knew Ethan would see the light at the end of the tunnel in one way or another. As they say, life happens when you're busy making other plans, and I was sure I'd learned what they meant the day I first ran into Ann in the supermarket.

THEY SAY FIND WHAT YOU LOVE AND LET IT KILL YOU. WELL, IT

works both ways. I finished off her Danish, and then I climbed the stairs to her bedroom. Eleven steps to the top. Six stab wounds. I had them all mapped out: one for each of the "accidents" I realized she was going to try and pin on me.

I didn't even get close to her with the knife.

"You're too chicken, Sadie," she said, and she was right. Turns out, I hate blood and open flesh. Turns out, I am weak. "When people are in love, they get predictable."

Ann knows this, so I know this.

That's why Ann and Paul are awake, waiting for me. She said I should have listened. She warned me they have cameras everywhere.

Together the two of them chloroformed me, took me to my house, where Paul later asphyxiated me in my bathroom.

The local headlines read: Devastated wife of child molester hangs herself.

But that wasn't even the half of it.

CHAPTER FORTY-THREE

HER

It's possible to make a murder look like a suicide, and it's possible to make a suicide look like murder. She was always going to be trouble. I knew it from the start. She isn't the first to fall in love with my wife. She's not the first to be obsessed. To get in the way. To not let go. Ann couldn't see it. Not like I did. She didn't want to tie that band around her neck and pull, pull, pull—so as usual, she left that part to me. She always leaves that part to me.

The problem is her heart. That's what Ann wanted right from the get-go. She got it. Just not in the way I thought.

Nothing with her went according to plan. Not with my wife begging me not to kill her—or rather warning me not to do it. And especially not with her handyman showing up, preventing me from finishing the job.

CHAPTER FORTY-FOUR

SADIE

Ann visits me in the hospital. I am shocked. Not only that she visits, but that I still have all of my organs, and they're mostly in working order.

There's damage to my larynx, which prevents me from speaking, and the injury to my left temporal lobe, given the asphyxiation, would probably affect my speech even if I could talk. The brain injury is supposed to affect my memory as well. But since I can't speak, well—no one knows for sure. This is why she visits.

This is why I'm not planning to let the doctors know what I know. My memory is just fine.

Supposedly, the situation to my larynx is temporary, but Ann says even if it weren't, there's a solution. She says they're making medical advances everyday. She says a transplant of the larynx is always a possibility.

When my room has emptied out, she tells me about everything I've missed. Amelia is a mess. A distraught teenage mess. Which is basically the worst kind. She thought she loved Ethan, Ann says. The way I thought I loved him.

Ann doesn't know what to do with her, so she sent her on one of those vacations where they take unruly teenagers into nature to sort themselves out. She'll be gone for twelve weeks. I've seen documentaries about those kind of trips. Didn't look like much of a vacation if you ask me.

Neil is as stoic as ever. Ann says he's growing more and more like his father every day. They plan to have him intern with Paul this summer. He's ready, she says.

She also speaks of the plans she has for Chet. She says she knows the reason I tried to commit suicide is partly his fault. She doesn't mention the death of my husband or the ensuing media coverage that is partly hers. It makes her look good to her fans that she visits me in the hospital. Forgiveness is a beautiful thing. It keeps her books flying off the shelves. She says Chet will be our secret. Forever and always. She says that nothing can ever come between us again.

I'm glad Ann visits, actually. She provides the motivation I need to mouth my first word since she choked them all out of me. *No.*

I can tell she's surprised by my reaction. This is a problem, she says to me. She says there is a remedy for all problems, and that if I'm not careful I will be at one with Ethan, Darcy, Darryl, and Creepy Stan. That, or I could end up like Kelsey. She tells me things have not turned out well for her.

When I look away and refuse to look at her—it's all I can really do to save myself in this condition—she apologizes.

She tells me not to worry about Chet. She says the good news is that his organs will be up for grabs, and maybe we'll meet up again, under different circumstances. She says donors' families often do that. She says his organs will be worth a lot. *Just think,* she tells me jubilantly, *someone out there will have his eyes, his heart. Imagine if the two of you fell in love. How romantic would that be?*

She says maybe I'll get lucky and find a man with Ethan's bones *and* Chet's skin, and that anything is possible. And even though I like the idea of Ethan's eyes and his heart and his skin being in and on someone else's body—even though I like the thought of him and Chet all mixed together so I get the best parts of both of them—I can't help but wonder where that leaves her. Is it really possible to have it all?

I close my eyes and think about it for a long time. When I open them again, it's like I am seeing things clearly for the first time and I know what I have to do. I know my angle.

She tells me she's sorry she's been so dreadful about everything. She was afraid she might lose me.

Just get better, Sadie, she says, and I want to. I really, really do. Our game depends on it.

After all, every love affair has its rituals—and you always kill what you love in the end.

CHAPTER FORTY-FIVE

HER

Accidental shocks are a very common thing. Particularly for an electrician. He was a lucky bastard. I wanted his death to be a little more instantaneous and a little less how do you say? *Leave-it-to-chance? Suspicious?*

Which is why he has to go out on a high note in life. Before the ravages of time and age make him more unappealing. While he is still young and virile enough to bang multiple women at one time.

Yes, I'm aware he fucked my wife.

Ann has her roundabout ways of making things happen, you see.

He had the wind at his back and the sun on his face. Or rather *in* his face. His car radio was blaring Stevie Ray as he rounded the corner at sixty miles an hour. By the time he spotted the deer, he had less than a millisecond to respond. Obviously, he chose poorly. Which wasn't surprising, given the choices he made in life. It was unlucky for him, his split- second decision both to avoid the deer and also fuck my wife. How could Sadie ever trust him after that, Ann wanted to know?

Not—how could I ever trust her.

And I certainly can't trust her.

But that doesn't stop me from loving her. Sex is sex. It's fairly mechanical, fairly short. Around eleven minutes on average. Ann and I have history. Real history. We made a commitment. Till death do us part. I intend to see it out. Which is why this fellow had to die. Loose ends are dangerous in surgery, and they are dangerous in a marriage.

Sadly, it wasn't even a real deer he swerved to avoid. Just a decoy, the kind hunters use to lure their prey. Although, by the time he realized that, if he had at all, he'd already hit the tree head on.

He didn't die on impact. Unfortunately. His truck was old, and without airbags, and still he held on. It's too bad he had an affinity for country roads and women who were off limits. The fast life, they call it. If only it hadn't taken someone so long to stop for help. If only the fire department hadn't had to work so hard to get him out. *If only. If only. If only.* If only, he might have lived.

CHAPTER FORTY-SIX

SADIE

I didn't see Ann run Chet off the road. But I am not surprised. Ann always has preferred her endings tidy and neat.

As she wheels me through the hospital doors, she tells me it's done. She says Chet is in the morgue downstairs, and it's almost pleasant to think of us in the same place once again.

She pushes me out into the courtyard; it's the perfect summer evening. As often as she can, considering her busy schedule, she comes to make sure I get to see the sunset. It's important, she says. Endings are often new beginnings in disguise.

She sets the brake on my wheelchair, and finally I get a good look at her. She looks radiant, as I expected she would, having just come from a book signing. Taking her in, I get that familiar pang deep down in the pit of my stomach. Sometimes you sense you are holding onto something meant to be let go. I get that sense now, but I'm careful to push the thought away just as soon as it comes.

Ann says it was like that with Ethan. She said I held on too long and it very nearly ruined me. Other times, she says, like with us, when you've found something spectacular, you find you can't let go. Sometimes if you've held something precious in your hands, in your heart, in your life—in all the places that count—you make sure you hold on tight. You do it because you know. You know what you have is so far beyond your wildest dreams that it would be nearly impossible to take anything less ever again. And what a shame it would be if you were made to; after all, the world can be a very mediocre place.

She has a point. Before Ann moved to Penny Lane, I was asleep. I was awake. But asleep. I was sleepwalking through life. But now I am awake, and now I can't stay angry, not so long as there's still so much to do. Not so long as the sun rises and it sets. Not so long as the future still holds so much promise. Not so long as I still have a shot at making things right.

And maybe it's crazy to think, but even if I could go back in time and know this was how it ended, I'd do it all again. I've been thinking a lot and I think that I could be the kind of stand-in parent Neil and Amelia need. I think motherhood could give me purpose. Sure, I hate teenagers. But I suppose I could get over that. I've already gotten over so much.

The doctors say I'm progressing well in therapy. A full recovery probably isn't a reality for me, but with the right therapies, I may be able to live on my own again. Ann says not to listen to them. She says doctors don't know everything. As usual, she says nothing is impossible.

The book signing was amazing, she tells me. Sold out, with a line out the door and around the corner. I smile in the only way I can these days: half-lipped and half-hearted.

I suppose I could be really bitter about the way it all unfolded. I could rage against what has happened to me. What I've become. Brain injuries are atrocious. Every day is two steps forward, one step back. But Ann is right. How can I stay mad, when the world is filled with so much beauty?

As we stare at the purples and the blues of a day gone by, Ann reminds me that life is about the journey, not the destination, and what a journey this has been.

Without the ability to speak, it sometimes feels like all of my other senses are heightened, like everything is coming at once. When it gets to be too much, as it often does, I press a little red button attached to my IV and into my bloodstream something magically goes to help me relax. I let go, and it's like I'm floating up, up, and away. It's like I stop trying to contain it all in the ball of my fist, and it flows through me like a river. Now is one of those times.

Ann asked me early on if I know what the three Ps are. I didn't then. But I learned. And now I know why. The three Ps are the key to any kind of success.

Passion: Without passion, you may as well forget your mission.

Patience: Patience enables you to stay the course even under the most difficult of circumstances.

Perseverance: Be persistent in pursuit of your goals and dreams.

Hope is not an option. It's imperative. The three Ps are the only choice, really. Anger will not get me what I want.

The good news is, Ann is working on getting me a voice box. It's difficult, because it has to be perfect. She says if I can't have my own voice, that I need to at least sound like me. She tells me not to worry when I seem impatient. Ann believes short cuts are the root of all evil.

Paul is making great advances, and someday, when I get out of here, we'll track down the man who got Ethan's eyes and Chet's heart. She says she plans to leave Paul —that the two of us can live and work together. She says it will be perfect, and even though I know it's not true, I can't help but feel nothing but appreciation for every single lovely little lie she tells.

As the sun sinks lower into the sky, and my eyelids grow heavy from the weight of the day and the drugs, Ann tells me it's a miracle we found each other on a planet of seven billion people. She says not to worry about any of it, she says the speech she gave tonight at her book signing was in honor of me. She told her fans not to spend a minute of their time worrying. Instead, she says we should focus on love and love alone. Love will see us through. We get one wild and precious life, and what a waste it would be not to realize what we have while we have it. She said, in the end we're all made of star dust, and to dust we shall return. *Ashes, ashes. We all fall down.*

As I drift off, she tells me they probably had no idea what she was talking about, which is probably for the best. Someday, they will.

CHAPTER FORTY-SEVEN

HER

S he wakes up on the operating table. I tell her not to worry, everything has gone according to plan. What I don't tell her is whose plan. I can't just yet—and, maybe not ever. It matters little anyhow. What's done is done. I inject something into her IV to help with the panic she is feeling. It's a scary thing to wake up tied down, in the dark, without your sight.

Although, fear does wonders for a relationship, I know this better than anyone. Still, I don't want her to be afraid.

"I'm sorry Sadie couldn't be here," I tell her softly. "She wanted to be. She really did. But you know how she feels about blood."

Ann is quite drowsy and it's unlikely she'll remember what I've told her later but just in case, I explain what's happened. "You shouldn't feel any pain? You'll let me know though won't you?"

Her expression is loose, and I know this is a positive sign. The drugs are working their magic. I pull the sheet up to her chest. Patients often complain of being cold when waking after anesthesia. "I know you're probably wondering what this is all about and to what extent. Well, darling, I've performed enucleation surgery."

Her vitals change. I watch the monitor for several seconds. Sometimes this can be a pain response. This time, I don't think so.

She does have some concept of what I'm saying. "I know you know this but I'm going to be thorough for the sake of being thorough. You know how I hate when details are left out. And I know how you hate loose ends. Although, I'm sure all of that is behind us now. Anyway—enucleation is the surgical removal of the eyeball, or in your case my love, both eyeballs. Not to worry though," I say patting her arm. "The muscles that were attached to the outside of the eyeball to control its movement and other tissues that surrounded your eye within the bony socket of the skull have been left intact. In time, if you're good, these muscles will be attached to a round, marble-like implant that will replace the tissue and volume lost. Attaching these muscles to the implant will offer some movement of the artificial eye after surgery."

I know that she isn't yet lucid enough to offer a response but I also know that she is worried about her appearance. My wife is always worried over her appearance and I want to put her at ease, so I say: For now, a small plastic conformer that resembles half an almond shell has been placed behind the eyelids to maintain their shape. In addition, a single stitch has been placed in your eyelids to temporarily sew them together. The conformer will serve as a placeholder for the artificial eye that, like I said, if you're good, will be fitted in a few weeks, after the swelling subsides. You'll understand that we need sufficient healing to take place before we discuss the next steps. The good news: I've picked out the perfect shade of green for your new eyes. You know how I've always loved green eyes. They're so rare and a redhead *really* should have green eyes. I know you'll like them. Even better, with a few modifications, your condition shouldn't affect your work inside the home. You can still manage the hotline and you can still write. We'll just have to keep you out of the public eye," I say pausing to clear my throat, "sorry for the pun. We'll have to keep you close to home for a bit—until the proper announcements can be made. You've suffered giant cell arteritis."

When I was summoned to Sadie's hospital room and she

handed me this wonderful little story of hers, I must say, it was quite eye-opening. I hadn't realized how many mistakes my wife had made. Sadie had video evidence I wouldn't want anyone to see, in addition to audio recordings from my home ready to be sent to the police. Ann was negligent. Incredibly so. Suffice it to say, I learned a lot. I learned that some things are hard to see until they're right up close and spelled out with ink.

The truth is, Ann invited her in. She invited a whole series of unfortunate circumstances upon our family. In a way, she asked for this. An eye for an eye, I suppose. Or in my wife's case, both eyes. Really, it's not like I had a choice.

It was one of Sadie's conditions. I tried to warn Ann about her. I tried to take care of the problem. But the problem just keeps coming back. As they say, love is blind.

Ann whimpers indicating the drugs are wearing off. She absently reaches for my hand and I let her have it. "I know you're confused," I whisper, smoothing her hair. She grips my hand, digging her nails into my skin. I take her hand from mine and force it to relax. I know what she's thinking the way you do when you've been with a person long enough. She doesn't recall what I've just told her. She's thinking, *what have you done?*

"Shhhh," I tell her, knowing how much she likes it when I read her mind. "I'll explain it all again in time."

In time, she'll ask why I didn't just kill Sadie Hightower. I could have. I could have done us all a favor and finally ridded my family of her all together. But something Sadie said made sense. She said this situation could help people. She said it could help Ann's career. It could show that we can all overcome things, no matter our circumstances. Partly, that is true. But something bigger and more profound occurred to me. Something I realized as I read her story.

My wife will never stop. If it weren't Sadie, it would always be someone else. Sadie is the lesser of all evils, so far as I'm concerned. At least with her, it isn't my wife she's in love with. It's the fame, the acknowledgement. The celebrity. The desire to be needed. The desire to not be left behind.

And now, with my wife blind, Sadie is needed. Without a doubt, Ann's life will be indefinitely more limited from this point forward. But it isn't the end of the world and as Sadie proposed, she is here to help with that.

I had to admit, her terms and conditions of not publishing the story, of not going to the police made sense, as skewed as it may sound. Sadie was right. Now, Ann can never leave me. Better yet, she'll be less likely to betray me again as well.

What can I say? Two birds, one stone.

EPILOGUE

I wish someone had told me: worry is a waste of time. The real troubles of your life will be things that never bothered to cross your mind. Nine months, three days, and nineteen hours, I've lived down the street from her. If you really think about it, a person can do a lot in nine months. They can gestate a fetus and deliver it safely into the world, and they can also plant roots and create an entirely different life altogether. That's what she did.

Not that I realized it at the time, but in essence, that's what she helped me do, too. What's good for the goose is good for the gander, as they say. Only she isn't a bird. She can't just fly away, the way she thinks she can.

She thinks she can migrate, start a new life elsewhere, some-place where she can be whatever she wants to be. In the heaviness of night, I know she is plotting her escape. Once I heard her whispering to Paul about moving back to the city where it would be easier for her.

Her recovery has been far worse than mine. Ann is angry. Combative. Paul has prescribed something for that. Sometimes she blames me and other times, it's him. Never herself.

I realized all along what drew Ann to me. Partly, I was just a pawn in the sick game she plays with Paul. Not so different than the one Ethan and I played.

With Ann though, it was different. She wanted me to be her endgame. She wanted to be absolved of responsibility. That's why she asked for my help. Again and again. She wanted me to be her mouthpiece. She wanted me to be her eyes and her ears, and now I am.

Obviously, this arrangement won't last forever. She thinks I don't know what she's plotting. She thinks I don't know what she's capable of. I know everything about her.

Also, she's forgetting two things: wherever you go, there you are. And, there are people like me.

When I moved to this boring, homogeneous, monotonous little town, I did so with one intention and one intention only: to have a nice life. A quiet life.

That's not how it played out. Not even close.

What can I say? I got swept up in it. She makes it easy. Her, with her impractical shoes and her perpetually sunny nature. For me, she has always felt a bit like spring in the middle of winter. She was then, and still is to me now, just about the most wonderful thing in the world.

But therein lies the problem. Nothing can last forever. And you always kill what you love in the end.

You do what you do. It is what it is.

You break wide open. Then you fix it.

Ann says we all have our own guidance system that lets us know what's right. It's there in the way we feel. She used to say that we can't blame other people for what happens to us, even if it feels good to do. There is truth in that, I suppose. Her next book, her last, the one she'll never finish, the one I've just finished reading talks about how we're all writing our own parts in the stories of our lives. We make deliberate choices that then represent the way our storyline goes.

She is so very right about that, and I have decided I can't go another minute without letting her know.

At the top of the stairs, I will find her in her bed, third door to the right. By this time of night, she will be sleeping on her side, covers pulled halfway up. Her expression will be slack, but peaceful, for even in sleep women like her know only ease.

On the left side of the four-poster bed is a nightstand. On top of the nightstand rests the Bible she doesn't read, the cell phone she'll never reach, a glass of water she'll never drink, the reading glasses she no longer needs.

I will attack from the right, stabbing her six times. I've mapped it out. Six stab wounds, one for each of the ways she has wronged me. In reality, it doesn't take that much to kill a person. She probably knows this better than anyone. And if not, just in case, I want to make sure.

This time it will be different. I'm like still water, lost in the process, minimizing the moment, under reacting to everything. It's not easy to get to this state. The hardest thing you can try to do is to be yourself when you're doing something you really care about. It takes discipline.

I've worked hard. I've been disciplined. I had lots of time, caring for her, and before that lying there in the hospital, and then afterward in the rehabilitation center. So much time. So many hours to fill. Every single second I've spent in therapy, I worked. Every time, I fed her or helped her learn to navigate her new condition, I planned. I learned to perform well despite nerves and the physical symptoms that accompany them—trembling, wet hands, rapid heartbeat, a sinking feeling in the gut, and sometimes even a feeling that breathing is difficult.

I feel all of this now.

Ann says these physical symptoms of nerves are the products of inevitable chemical changes that occur inside the body during moments of high stress, changes like a shot of adrenaline. They're outside our conscious control. So it's a waste of time trying to avoid them.

Thankfully, this time, I don't have to. She will not be surprised to find me in her room tonight. I am her caretaker. I am her children's caretaker.

Paul is out of town again, as he so often is. Ann likes me to sleep in her room whenever he's away, and tonight is no different. Sometimes we touch our own wounds to be punished. Still, she worries about him, I know. But as I lift the covers to her right and lean into Paul's side of the bed, she sleeps soundly.

Until she isn't. "Sadie?" she calls. "Is that you?"

When I don't answer, she rolls over to make room for me and pats the mattress. "Come to bed, Sadie," she whispers, her voice thick with sleep. "I've just had the best idea, and I want to tell you every little thing."

I climb into bed and tuck the knife underneath the mattress. I live for Ann's stories. I'm in love with her ideas. Especially when I get to take credit for them. Every love affair has its rituals. As she curls her warm body around mine, I think of the knife and I tell myself maybe tomorrow. But tomorrow usually turns out just the same.

A NOTE FROM BRITNEY

Dear Reader,

I hope you enjoyed reading *HER*. If you have a moment and you'd like to let me know what you thought, feel free to drop me an email. I enjoy hearing from readers.

Writing a book is an interesting adventure, it's a bit like inviting people into your brain to rummage around. *Look where my imagination took me. These are the kind of stories I like...*

That feeling is often intense and unforgettable. And mostly, a ton of fun.

With that in mind—thank you again for reading my work. I don't have the backing or the advertising dollars of big publishing, but hopefully I have something better... readers who like the same kind of stories I do. If you are one of them, please share with your friends and consider helping out by doing one (or all) of these quick things:

1. Visit my Review Page and write a 30 second review (even short ones make a big difference).

(http://britneyking.com/aint-too-proud-to-beg-for-reviews/)

Many readers don't realize what a difference reviews make but they make ALL the difference.

2. Drop me an email and let me know you left a review. This way I can enter you into my monthly drawing for signed paperback copies.

(britney@britneyking.com)

3. Point your psychological thriller loving friends to their <u>free copies</u> of

my work. My favorite friends are those who introduce me to books I might like. **(http://www.britneyking.com)**

4. If you'd like to make sure you don't miss anything, to receive an email whenever I release a new title, sign up for my New Release Newsletter. **(https://britneyking.com/new-release-alerts/)**

Thanks for helping, and for reading my work. It means a lot.

Britney King

Austin, Texas

April 2018

ABOUT THE AUTHOR

Britney King lives in Austin, Texas with her husband, children, two dogs, one ridiculous cat, and a partridge in a peach tree.

When she's not wrangling the things mentioned above, she writes psychological, domestic and romantic thrillers set in suburbia.

Without a doubt, she thinks connecting with readers is the best part of this gig. You can find Britney online here:

Email: britney@britneyking.com
Web: https://britneyking.com
Facebook: https://www.facebook.com/BritneyKingAuthor
Instagram: https://www.instagram.com/britneyking_/
Twitter: https://twitter.com/BritneyKing_
Goodreads: https://bit.ly/BritneyKingGoodreads
Pinterest: https://www.pinterest.com/britneyking_/

Happy reading.

ACKNOWLEDGMENTS

As always thank you to my family and friends for the endless ways you provide love and inspiration.

Thank you to my friends in the book world. From bloggers to my editor to all of the people I'm lucky enough to do business with—you make this gig so much fun.

To my beta readers and my advance reader team... there aren't enough words to describe the appreciation I feel for you—for being my biggest cheerleaders. To Jenny Hanson and Samantha Wiley, thank you.

Last, but certainly not least, many thanks to the readers. I always say the best part of writing, for me, is the relationship I have with readers. Readers are the bee's knees. Thank you for being that.

ALSO BY BRITNEY KING

The Social Affair | Book One

The Replacement Wife | Book Two

Speak of the Devil | Book Three

The New Hope Series Box Set

The New Hope Series offers gripping, twisted, furiously clever reads that demand your attention, and keep you guessing until the very end. For fans of the anti-heroine and stories told in unorthodox ways, *The New Hope Series* delivers us the perfect dark and provocative villain. The only question—who is it?

Water Under The Bridge | Book One

Dead In The Water | Book Two

Come Hell or High Water | Book Three

The Water Series Box Set

The Water Trilogy follows the shady love story of unconventional married couple—he's an assassin—she kills for fun. It has been compared to a crazier book version of Mr. and Mrs. Smith. Also, Dexter.

Bedrock | Book One

Breaking Bedrock | Book Two

Beyond Bedrock | Book Three

The Bedrock Series Box Set

The Bedrock Series features an unlikely heroine who should have known better. Turns out, she didn't. Thus she finds herself tangled in a messy, dangerous, forbidden love story and face-to-face with a madman hell-bent on revenge. The series has been compared to Fatal Attraction, Single White Female, and Basic Instinct.

Around The Bend

Around The Bend, is a heart-pounding standalone which traces the journey of a well-to-do suburban housewife, and her life as it unravels, thanks to the secrets she keeps. If she were the only one with things she wanted to keep hidden, then maybe it wouldn't have turned out so bad. But she wasn't.

Somewhere With You | Book One

Anywhere With You | Book Two

The With You Series Box Set

The With You Series at its core is a deep love story about unlikely friends who travel the world; trying to find themselves, together and apart. Packed with drama and adventure along with a heavy dose of suspense, it has been compared to The Secret Life of Walter Mitty and Love, Rosie.

SNEAK PEEK: WATER UNDER THE BRIDGE

BOOK ONE

In the spirit of *Gone Girl* and *Behind Closed Doors* comes a gripping, twisting, furiously clever read that demands your attention, and keeps you guessing until the very end. For fans of the anti-heroine and stories told in unorthodox ways, *Water Under The Bridge* delivers us the perfect dark and provocative villain.

As a woman who feels her clock ticking every single moment of the day, former bad girl Kate Anderson is desperate to reinvent herself. So when she sees a handsome stranger walking toward her, she feels it in her bones, there's no time like the present. *He's the one.*

Kate vows to do whatever it takes to have what she wants, even if that something is becoming someone else. Now, ten pounds thinner, armed with a new name, and a plan, she's this close to living the perfect life she's created in her mind.

But Kate has secrets.

And too bad for her, that handsome stranger has a few of his own.

With twists and turns you won't see coming, Water Under The Bridge examines the pressure that many women feel to "have it all" and introduces a protagonist whose hard edges and cutthroat ambition will leave you questioning your judgment and straddling the line between what's right and wrong.

Enjoy dark fiction? Are you a fan of stories told in unique ways? If so, you'll love Britney King's bestselling psychological thrillers. Get to know Jude and Kate, unreliable narrators at best, intense, and, in your face at worst. *Water Under The Bridge* is the first book in The Water Trilogy. Available in digital and print.

DEAD IN THE WATER (Book Two) and COME HELL OR HIGH WATER (Book Three) are now available.

What readers are saying:

"Another amazingly well-written novel by Britney King. It's every bit as dark, twisted and mind twisting as Water Under The Bridge...maybe even a little more so."

"Hands down- best book by Britney King. Yet. She has delivered a difficult writing style so perfectly and effortlessly, that you just want to worship the book for the writing. The author has managed to make murder/assassination/accidental- gunshot- to-the-head-look easy. Necessary."

"Having fallen completely head over heels for these characters and this author with the first book in the series, I've been pretty much salivating over the thought of this book for months now. You'll be glad to know that it did not disappoint!"

Series Praise

"If Tarantino were a woman and wrote novels... they might read a bit like this."

"Fans of Gillian Flynn and Paula Hawkins meet your next obsession."

"Provocative and scary."

"A dark and edgy page-turner. What every good thriller is made of."

"I devoured this novel in a single sitting, absolutely enthralled by the storyline. The suspense was clever and unrelenting!"

"Completely original and complex."

"Compulsive and fun."

"No-holds-barred villains. Fine storytelling full of mystery and suspense."

"Fresh and breathtaking insight into the darkest corners of the human psyche."

WATER UNDER THE BRIDGE

BRITNEY KING

COPYRIGHT

Hot Banana Press
Cover Design by Britney King LLC
Cover Image by Grant Reid Photography
Copy Editing by Librum Artis Editorial Services &
RMJ Manuscript Services
Proofread by Proofreading by the Page

First Edition: 2016
ISBN: 978-0-9966497-2-8 (Paperback)
ISBN: 978-0-9966497-4-2 (All E-Books)
britneyking.com

For the Lovers—
for there are few things as easy or as hard as loving.

PREFACE

There's a girl long dead who rests down by the water's edge.
Her final words were, "No. Don't. Please. I'm sorr—."
She never did get the second half of her apology out.
I made sure she never will.
Some things are best left unsaid, I think.
In the end, it didn't matter.
I knew she was sorry.
And she knew it too.

~

There's a girl who rests down by the water's edge.
She was beautiful, but you and the water washed it all away.
You think I don't know what you've done, but I do.
I know that you visit on occasion, and I know other things too.

~

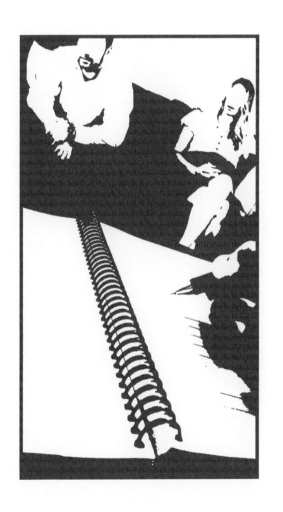

CHAPTER ONE

JUDE

AFTER

Your face crumbles as the judge hands down our sentence. I am fascinated by the way your expression changes, as slowly, recognition takes over that unlike the rest of your affairs, this one isn't going to be a one-and-done deal. Turns out, lucky us, the great State of Texas is having a go at a pilot program designed to drop the state's divorce rate.

But you aren't feeling very lucky. Not at all. I can tell by the way you pinch the bridge of your nose. You've always hated not getting your way. It doesn't matter anyway. I want to tell you—whatever political agenda bullshit this latest program entails—I can assure you and the rest of Texas, it won't save us. Even if I were the kind of man who believed in miracles, you and me, we'd need a miracle plus a Hail Mary. You've said it yourself, where we are concerned, there is no hope. And this is why you plead.

"Excuse me, your Honor—," you start, and you pause for effect, always the performer. "This really isn't necessary," you profess and then you swallow, and I like it when you're unsure. You go on. "My hus—Jude and I—," you tell him, and you look over at me, and my god, Kate, you've always done indifference so well. "I think we can both agree we're ready to get on with our lives."

You refer to me as your husband—or almost, anyway—and for a moment, I recall what it felt like before your words were laced with poison, back when there was nothing but hope.

I listen to you say your piece, and this time is no different than all the times before, only this time, we have witnesses, and you know how I've always hated that. You must know this because you sink back in your chair, proud.

Your pride doesn't last long because when the judge lists out the terms of our captivity, you glare at your attorney, willing her to save you, but she won't—she can't. You almost choke when he orders six months of marriage counseling, which includes weekly appointments. Your hand flies to your throat, and I remember what that's like, holding you in place, having it all in the palm of my hand. I'd give anything—maybe even your life—to know what that feels like again.

The good news here is the judge and I seem to be on the same page as he informs the two of us that a therapist of our choosing must sign off before the court will grant our divorce. You hold your breath as he speaks, and I remember what that felt like too.

I try, for you, though... I do. I wait for him to finish, and then I tell him that you're right, we've made our decision, and as I speak, you sulk, but isn't this what you've always wanted, to be right? It's hard to look at you, sulking or otherwise, and it never used to be this way.

You're tanner than the last time I saw you. But then, I guess time away did you good. You said you needed your space, and I let you have it. But you have to know, Kate, it was hard not to follow. Maybe I should have. But it was all the same to you—you made up your mind, and your decision settled mine.

Nevertheless, if there is such a thing as a clean break for you and me, it isn't looking good, and it certainly won't be handed down today. This judge does not cease his interminable vendetta against your freedom. He does not relent. You aren't happy, and I can't recall the last time you were, even though I try. It'll come to me, the memory of you, but this courtroom is too stuffy, and you know how I've always hated an audience.

The judge looks away, and you look on, defeated; it's clear, even if you refuse to let it show. As he jots something down, you bite your lip, a tell—you still believe there's hope. But I know better. When he looks up, holding a pen and our future in his hands, you tell him you'd be better off dead, and he looks surprised, as though he's missed something. He has. A lot of somethings. He asks if there's a history of violence. No, you tell him, it was just an expression. Although a part of me wonders if you're right about that too. Maybe there's truth in what you say. Maybe you would be better off dead, and I can't help but wonder if I have it in me.

~

YOU TEXT, AND THERE'S SOMETHING ABOUT SEEING YOUR NAME light up my phone that still gets me even after all this time. You're all business with your words, and I remember how much I've always liked this side of you. You write that our first therapy session is on Tuesday, and it's so like you to take control, so like you to try and set the pace. But you are mistaken, Kate. Our first therapy session is Monday, and you seem to forget that I'm always one step ahead. You cease with the texting and ring me instead because you like to be the one calling the shots. You're ready to pounce when I offer formalities I don't mean—meanwhile, I'm just happy to hear your voice. You sound exasperated, and I wish I could see your face. No one tells you how much you can miss a person's face. You rattle off instructions, but we don't talk about things, not really, and I wonder when we stopped talking.

We're talking now, that's what you'd say. But I won't— because no one's really saying anything. Nothing worth saying, anyway.

Eventually, after I've refused to take the bait because I won't give you my anger as freely as you give yours, you relent, and you agree to the Monday appointment. You'd never admit it, but you like it when I put you in your place. Better to get it over with, you tell me with an edge. The sooner to see you, my dear, I think. But I don't say this. I give you what you want. I always have.

YOU SIT CROSS-LEGGED WITH YOUR HANDS FOLDED NEATLY IN YOUR lap, and I hate how pretty you look. Your hair is up, neat and orderly, different, and I study that spot on your neck, the one I know so well. It's your weak spot, and given the chance, I'd dive right in. But we're here, not there, in more ways than one, and I hate that this middle-aged doctor is checking you out. I don't know why you had to wear such a low-cut top, and I recognize the look he gives you. He has a weakness too. But he thinks he's the one in charge here—I can tell by the way he wears it via the chip on his shoulder—when, in reality, he lacks a real MD behind his name. He'd better watch himself. I'll kill him if I have to. He isn't old, the way I'd imagined, and I silently curse myself for not doing more research on something so important.

"Dr. C." That's how he introduces himself, and it's clear he's the kind of fellow who believes in make-believe. What a joke this is—what a joke he is. We would laugh about this, you and I, if things were different. If now were before. But it isn't, and no one's laughing.

"So...why don't you tell me where things went wrong...?" he urges, and I want to hate him, and I almost do, but I admire his directness. I, too, am eager to get to the point.

You shrug, and then I do the same because I'm well-versed in the art of mirroring, but mostly because I want to know your answer. I'm glad he starts here because he doesn't know us, Kate, this fake doctor. He doesn't know that other doctors (both real and fake) have told us we're not capable of love. But we were capable, you and I. We were. We weren't make-believe like this guy. We didn't pretend we were something we weren't until we did—and that is the real reason we're here, but I don't say this. I let you lead the way.

"Is there really any way to know, Doc—" you start and then you stop. You don't call him 'doctor,' but you let him think he's in charge, and I like that you're on to him, too. You know his ability to ask a good question doesn't make him a real doctor, and this is a good start. Already, we're getting somewhere, you and I, and I'm starting to feel something that looks a lot like hope.

You are right, I tell him. There's really no way of knowing where things went bad, no way to pinpoint exactly who's at fault, and yet here we are, sitting in these chairs, talking to him instead of each other, both wanting nothing more than to be anywhere else, getting on with our lives.

You nod, and we're on the same page again, and all of a sudden the world seems less bleak.

He asks how we met, and you crinkle your nose.

"Does it really matter?" I ask. "It's over," I say. "Isn't it best to let it be?" I add for good measure, showing that I, too, can ask good questions. You sit up a little straighter, but you drop your guard.

"Perhaps," he says, even though he and I both know he doesn't mean it. *Perhaps.* Give me a break. He doesn't know how much I hate that word, but you do, and I see the corners of your lips turn upward as he says it. It doesn't matter, though. He isn't fooling me with his half-hearted response. 'Dr. C' is a man used to being right. He likes control, he likes being in charge, he gets off on toying with people's emotions, and perhaps I could show him the error of his ways.

"And yet—," he adds, as though he's exasperated when he hardly knows what it means to lift a finger, "I want to go back to where it began." He speaks to me as he looks at you, and I can't blame him. They say living well is the best form of revenge. They are right, and in this case, it's pretty apparent—I am bad at revenge.

"I think it would be a good idea for the two of you to tell each other the story of your coming together—in writing," he says, looking from you to me and back, and I can't be mad at him for staring at your tits when he has such good ideas. "I find writing helps clients come to terms with the dissolution of their marriage in a way that merely talking doesn't…" he continues, pausing for added effect, and you cross your arms. "Writing can be reflective. I find it helps my clients to move on, and more importantly, it lends to healthier relationships in the future."

"I don't write," you tell him, as you shift in your seat—you little liar, you. You write all the time.

"You wrote the text you sent me about this very appointment," I say because he needs to know those tits he's staring at are *my* tits and that we still talk. You give me that look, the one I know so well, and perhaps you are onto me.

"Just give it a try," the fake doctor insists, adjusting his glasses on his nose, and I'd pay money to prove they aren't even prescription. "Trust me," he says, and I don't. I hope you don't either. "It'll save the two of you time talking to me," he adds. It's a small offer of condolence, and thankfully, he says something I like. Only this guy doesn't know you like I do. He may have me convinced, but he hasn't convinced you, and you are not soothed. I can tell by the way you check your phone every two and a half seconds. You're distracted, and you don't trust him. You don't want to talk to him, and I hate that phone for getting more of you than you give to us.

"What happens if I just don't come back?" you ask, and this isn't a threat—you genuinely want to know. You, always the stubborn one, always the one to test the limits, until suddenly, you just don't.

"Well—" he says, and I can tell you've tested him. He's intrigued by your defiance, and I will squash him if he gets any ideas…just like I will squash that phone of yours if you don't stop staring at it. "It's mandatory if you want to wrap up your divorce," he tells you, and I like the direction he's going. I like that he plays hardball, so I don't have to. "Furthermore, you'd be violating a court order, and of course, that's not something I'd advise."

You look over at me, and I smile, and you are so clever. You're not the kind of girl who enjoys being backed against the wall— until you are, and that's exactly what I'm imagining doing right now. I think he is too, and perhaps I'll let it slide, but only because I can tell by your expression you understand he's forcing you to come back here, back to me.

"Fine," you say, and it's too bad you're not a mind reader.

"I'll give it a try," you tell him, and you sigh. You check your phone again, and this is a new one, but then, you've always surprised me with your intelligence. You look up, only this time not at me, and I get that familiar pain in my chest I know all to well. "Now, can I go?" you ask, raising your brow, and you're ready to pounce if the answer that comes isn't the one you want.

"Yes," he says, and you stand. You're about to bolt when he stops you with the flick of a wrist, and I remember when I could do that. "That is—if you agree, Jude. I need a commitment here that you'll both come prepared with something in hand by our next appointment," he adds, and there's authority in his voice when he speaks. You wait, and you listen, and this isn't the girl I know. He's looking at me now as though he and I are on the same team. We aren't, and he can't know how much you both love and hate authority, and maybe this is the answer to his question about where it all went wrong.

"Sure," I tell him, offering my best smile. "I'll come up with something for you, Doc," I offer as though I'm his star student, when in fact, I'm full of shit. But he buys it, and you are antsy because you know I've won. "I'll write you a whole book, if that's what it takes," I add for good measure. He smiles. "I'll call it Water Under the Bridge," I say, fucking with you. You shake your head at me. Then you roll your eyes and start for the door. I'm pretty sure you know he's checking out your ass, and he'd better watch himself. There was a time when this wouldn't have bothered me, a time when I believed in you... when I believed in us.

Now is not that time.

∼

Learn more at: britneyking.com

54396490R00156

Made in the USA
Middletown, DE
13 July 2019